Nothing To Fear

BK Wells
www.bkwells.com

Nothing To Fear

Table of Contents

Chapter 1

Jedidiah Butts was fat. Rolls of flab piled over his belt buckle, and with every step in the slush, he felt the blubber slap against itself, bouncing and slapping, flesh against flesh. What was the sound of one stomach clapping? He listened. That was the sound. The weight of his gut cut into the metal belt buckle. Why did he have three eggnogs? And five frosted brownies. He could have just eaten the frosting, or the brownie, but, no, he had to eat the frosting and the beautiful, crumbly, cakey, cocoa brownie. And every bite had been heaven. But now, as he felt his belly hang over his belt, he was having snacker's remorse.

His briefcase was heavy too, and it slapped his upper thigh with every other step. The cold stiffened his shoulder and his bad knee. He should've taken a cab, but he wanted to see it before he went home. In the last block, the slush turned into crunchy snow, and with every step, he heard the sound of the snow crunching under the sole of his wingtips. It sounded like the mouthfuls of corn chips he'd eaten. Why so many? Why couldn't he stop? Chips were the most comforting food—the hammering crush pulverizing the chips, the sound echoing and reverberating in his brain, the relief delivered by the grinding and gnashing of the little corn or potato beauties. Those ranch chips, the corn ones, were especially good. How many? He'd probably eaten at least half a bag, but not a whole bag. Why the guacamole? He'd been so good and now this one night of recklessness. It was the holidays, and everyone needed a little splurge now and then, plus, the office only had one holiday party. Would his poor choice unravel his blood pressure, diabetes, or gout? His doctor was going to kill him.

He stopped, looked up, and there it was, as majestic as the first time he'd seen it. The White House. He was looking at it through the fence, but every time he saw the fabulous dome, he couldn't believe it was real and that he was here, in Washington D.C.

Congressman Butts thought back to when he was a boy, growing up in Atlanta. With so many changes over the decades, the hometown of his youth was just a dream. It was as if he'd been a completely different person. Actually, he *had* been a different person. A child. A child with an insatiable craving. When he thought of those days, he always drifted back to one event.

There had been a snow globe at the local Woolworth's. Every day he could get to it, he would go in and look at the snow globe, shake it and watch the snow float around the White House. This was a real glass snow globe on a wooden base. Inside was a little carved White House. Why of all things it had The White House in it and why someone thought the Woolworth's in Atlanta would be able to sell it, who knew. But he would go into the store and head straight to it. He'd pick it up—it seemed huge but that was only because his hands had been so small. He would hold it and stare at it, his little boy brain traveling in a hypnotic fog, and he would dream that one day he'd walk past those columns and into that house. Shaking that glass globe and watching the little flakes tumble and float, he had imagined himself as the president. He was the president, and he had on a fancy suit and a top hat, and, with his arms out like bird, he would fly from room to room. Every room was huge and furnished like a palace. He would float through the presidential palace like the snowflakes gliding through the water.

He'd be president, and he'd sit in a big chair and eat pancakes for every meal, and he'd make things equal for everybody. He'd change the name of the White House and call it the Equal House. And he'd paint it blue, so no one would think it was just for white people anymore. And he would fly like a bird in his fancy suit, circling the Equal House. He'd be the richest man, and he'd have enough money to give anyone anything they wanted. For example, if a boy in Atlanta needed five dollars for a snow globe, President Butts would fly there in his fancy suit and give him the five dollars.

He had spent hours gazing in that glass ball. Oh, the pleasure and joy that had come from that innocent daydream. Of course, he'd been followed by the floorwalker, though, after a while, even he had given up on the boy. Then, one day in December, a day like this, he had hidden the snow globe under his coat and walked out of Woolworth's, an eight-year-old with a spare tire. The second he'd gotten out of the store, the Woolworth's floorwalker had come up behind him and dragged him back into the store. Butts didn't know how, but within the hour, his mother had appeared, and the man told her Jedidiah was a thief. "I'm not a thief. I just wanted it."

"You can't just have everything you want," the Woolworth had man said.

"I NEEDED it," corrected Butts.

"Why did you need this?" asked the Woolworth's man with a nod to the globe.

"Because I'm going to be president." Even as a child, he'd easily deciphered the telling glance between his mother and the floorwalker. They didn't believe he could be president. Even today, Butts recalled the burn of shame on his cheeks. They hadn't believed him. The floorwalker had let him go, no doubt on account of foolishness instead of maliciousness. Years later, he'd realized that glance hadn't been that HE couldn't be president, it was that no black man could be president. *One day, that will change,* thought Butts on this winter day.

Butts chuckled. His mom had bought the snow globe and made him chop wood for a month. Five dollars was a lot of money, and she was darn-tootin' he would pay his debt. She'd never told his father, and his father had passed not long after. His mother was just, yet kind. A good woman. Yes, his mother, God rest her soul, was a good, good woman. It amused him now to think that he had wanted something so badly that he was willing to steal it. That snow globe had represented escape, equality, a dream. He'd wanted to steal equality. Butts smiled at his own precociousness. He was still willing to steal to get it.

He had come a long way from the Atlanta Woolworth's, and it had been a long, challenging road. He'd been part of the civil rights movement as a teen, had gone to law school, defended civil rights from the bench, run for Congress and had the privilege of serving in office. His life had been the American Dream, yet after all those years of fantasizing about the White House, when he'd actually arrived and saw it, it couldn't beat his dreams. The White House in his head had been much more majestic. The little White House in the little globe seemed so much more brilliant. Shaking that globe had made him feel everything would turn out all right. His teacher had said, "Anyone can grow up to be president," and Butts believed it. He learned the truth later. Maybe not just anyone could be the president, but anyone could lead. Anyone could serve. Butts believed that with his whole heart. Every citizen was a member of this community, everyone was welcome at the table, to bring an idea, or voice an issue. Anyone could lead. Look at him—his parents had been dirt poor, his father a sharecropper, his mother a domestic. His great-grandparents had been slaves. And he, Jedidiah Butts, was a congressman. Anyone could be a leader. Everyone should be.

Light snow began to fall, and Butts cupped his hand and held it in front of him, once again holding the White House globe, this time as an adult, this time with the real White House. He thought of that little boy, so full of dreams that he was willing to compromise his beliefs and steal, and he

6

smiled. Fantasy or reality, he was here, and the Christmas season would officially start tonight. He would love to go see the lighting of the tree, watch the magical look on the faces of the children, feel the spark of hope in the hearts of all.

A snowflake landed on his mustache, and he wiped it away. The wetness, the cold—it reminded him he was alive. That's why he'd wanted to walk through the snow, dammit. He was alive. He'd survived prostate cancer and a mild heart attack. He had survived. He had continued. This would be the third Christmas without Bessie. He missed her. There were no words that could capture that pain. People are born, people die... it wasn't that simple. He would take flowers to Bessie's grave tomorrow—roses. A dozen red roses against the white snow.

He looked up again at the White House, and for one split second, he was that boy again, shaking his White House snow globe, a boy with no clue how he would end up here, but with a desire to serve this country. Somewhere, there was another boy or girl out there, unprepared, unaware that he or she would step up to serve the union. He sighed and smiled. Tomorrow—the challenges and the triumphs—belonged to the future.

He reached in his pocket and took out his pocket watch. It was a worn, gold-plated watch. The cover was decorated with a globe and crosshatching, and over the years of being opened and closed, the etching had worn away at an angle from the thumb sliding down the center. He would love to see them light the tree, or maybe go shopping for a new snow globe that he could keep in his study. But right now he had no time for amusement, he'd already spent three hours at a Christmas party, and he had a briefcase of work that needed to be completed by tomorrow. He moved the brief from under his arm to his chest and continued.

A worker leaned from a hydraulic lift and replaced a blown bulb. Below, another worker yelled at him, telling him what to do while the other workers stood around, ready to knock off. The lift lowered as light snow began to fall. The bulb-snatcher traveled down, twenty feet, ignoring the fresh, blue needles, the scent of the pine, and the sparkle of excitement that followed every Christmas Tree. But this was no ordinary tree, it was the grandest of pines, the National Christmas Tree, and it would stand proud, decorating not just the White House, but shining for every person in the United States. A crowd was already gathering, anticipating the lighting.

Press Secretary Jim Donaldson moved away from the window. He looked at President John Reed. Donaldson was fifty-five and felt every day of it. Reed was five years older than he was, yet the man was a whirlwind of action. Reed was always doing ten things at once. Would he ever slow down? Donaldson watched as Reed spooned a few mouthfuls of soup, checked his watch, made minor changes on typewritten sheets, and re-knotted his tie. He puffed out his chest, showing Donaldson the tie, and said, "Finished. How do I look, Jim?"

Donaldson looked at him. He couldn't deny the job had aged Reed... hell, it had aged him too. He looked at the bags under Reed's eyes and thought, *paper or plastic*?

"A little touch-up under the eyes, and they'll swear you just stepped out of Yale."

Reed squirted some breath freshener and headed out the door. He said, "Good. The youth thing."

Donaldson followed Reed out and said, "That's why you have a VICE president!

On another floor, Vice President J. Junior Worthy was hard at work in his office. He sat on a Twister mat spread across the floor. Junior had one hand on red, the other on blue, one sock on green and one sock on blue. His aide, Chet, manned the spinner.

Junior was more than ten years younger than Reed and showed none of the signs of exhaustion that came with the top job. He was handsome, charismatic, downright cute. Junior had a boyish charm, including a cowlick that would never take a rest. A splash of his brown hair dangled over one eye, and he was constantly pitching his head back to clear his view, like a teenager.

Chet was pure nerd—a skinny African American, a mustache, a suit, and a pair of hornrims. As a child, Chet had been good and had always done as he was told. He'd grown into an adult version of that child.

Junior rarely got a song right, but that never stopped him from trying. "Milton Someone something, something, something! Twist the twister, twist a dot, it twists you up a heckuva lot. Twister! Twister!" Wrong words, wrong tune as he tried to remember the commercial from his childhood. He stopped singing and looked at how he'd become a human pretzel.

"It did tie me up in a knot! How am I gonna get out of this one? Dad!" He chuckled. "What's next?"

Chet flicked the plastic arrow and it zipped around in a half dozen circles then stopped. "Left hand yellow."

Junior looked from hand to hand. "Wedding ring—left! This game can be so confusing!"

He curled around and carefully placed his left hand on a yellow dot. In his Republican issue suit, he looked like a Brooks Brothers contortionist. He touched near his heart. He could feel it through his suit. The medal. The indigo heart. His real

Daddy had won it in the army. When Junior had the indigo heart with him, he knew things would work out.

Chet said, "Don't you have anything more important than a game?"

"What could be more important than Twister?"

"How about reading through those intelligence briefs?"

"Uh, no," Junior said. "C'mon, Chet. If you play, I'll put in a good word to get you that Secretary of State job."

"You said that last week."

"These executive... whatever-you-call-its take time!"

On the ground floor, Donaldson and Reed briskly walked through the hall. Donaldson was trim, gray, and stoic. Reed was a no-nonsense Republican, one that always smiled but was never happy. He said, "Where is Junior, anyway? He better not be late."

"I still can't believe you got saddled with that bozo. We've got to get rid of him."

"I'd like to get rid of his father, too."

"'The congressman from Kalamazoo!' Give me a freaking break!" Donaldson often thought, but was always careful to not use, heavy expletives in front of the president or the media, choosing freaking or fricken' or fudging instead of the real deal. Reed never cursed either, so he never reacted to square language like freaking.

"It's amazing, but Fletcher Worthy is an even bigger asshole than his kid," Reed said. Asshole was acceptable. Coarse but not obscene.

"You must've owed him a big one, John."

"You knock up somebody's wife and see what it gets you. And I had to pay for the abortion!"

"I'm telling you, we gotta dump Junior. Way before the convention even starts. His presence is a knee in the groin of your administration."

"We'll give him the axe as soon as the holidays are over. Let's get our best people on this so it doesn't look like we're splitting the party."

"Health problem. That always works. Nobody questions a health resignation," said Donaldson. "That, or he wants to spend more time with his family. That indicates standard issue screwup."

"Anything! Just so we're not stuck with Junior."

"Can you imagine if that ignoramus ever became president?"

"Perish the thought," Reed said.

"This country would go to hell in a handbag. Then he'd let somebody steal the handbag!"

"You'd think this country would put a little more thought into who they elect."

And so, it was decided, as most deals were, in casual conversation, walking down a hall. Junior was as good as gone.

Chapter 2

Junior was trying to put his right hand across his torso, reaching for a red dot. Chet noticed the time. "Hey! You're gonna miss the lighting of the Christmas tree!"

Junior fell into a pile. "Oh no!" Junior looked at his watch. "Shoot!" He yelled at his watch. "A fie on you, Mickey! Let's go!"

The dynamic duo ran out the door. Junior said, "Do you think Santa REALLY knows when you've been naughty and nice? If he does, I've got buckos to pay! What's a fie, anyway?"

The small crowd had multiplied, and the bodies wriggled and writhed like earthworms unearthed in a clump of sod. To Reed, they were all worms, fresh bait to land his next big whopper—revising the Social Security system. It would look like he was making all the right choices for those worms when, really, he was firmly pushing them down on a double-pronged hook.

President Reed waved to the crowd then spoke to Donaldson. "There they are. *'The people.'* Every time I see 'em, it moves me a little. My heart skips a beat, I get a tear in my eye, and I think—Suckers!"

Reed and Donaldson chuckled together. They walked to a large platform decorated in holiday trimmings where they joined Mrs. Reed. Mrs. Reed was white haired, heavyset, and bug-eyed. Though a year younger, she looked old enough to be President Reed's mother. His HGH injections had been worth every penny.

The Second Lady, Caroline Worthy, stood next to Mrs. Reed. Caroline was prim to the point of prudishness. Mrs. Worthy wore a stylish 1940s suit, one more outfit from her endless collection of beige. Unfortunately, while her back was turned, the rest of the planet had stepped into the next millennium. Caroline glanced around, looking for Junior, who was nowhere in sight. She bit down hard on her tight, wrinkled, bottom lip.

Reed turned to her. "Where is he?"

Caroline tried not to reveal her worry and shrugged. "He said he had to finish something important."

"What? His bubble bath? Five bucks says he was playing Twister again."

Mrs. Reed played important roles—First Lady, dignitary, ambassador, but most important was her work mediating between her husband and the Second Lady. "Knock it off, you two. The esspray can earhay." She smiled and waved even more enthusiastically, a goofy grin on her chubby face.

Santa pulled up in a sleigh pulled by real reindeer. He climbed on the rostrum and waved to the crowd. "Ho, ho, ho!" Santa bellowed. The crowd screamed and applauded.

Reed pulled Santa by his fuzzy red sleeve. "I'm not gonna be upstaged by some two-bit Kris Kringle. You weren't supposed to show until the end of my speech." Both Reed and Santa smiled and waved like they were having the times of their lives. Under his breath Santa said, "Eat me, frat boy. I'm a Democrat."

Reed stepped up to the podium. He cleared his throat. "Happy Holidays! Welcome my fellow Americans. In my three years in office, this is the most spectacular tree I've had the fortune to light. Christmas is a special time—a magic time. A time when we all come together as human beings, put aside our minor differences, and show how much we really care." From the crowd, a sniper took a potshot at Reed. Reed saw the shot coming and dodged, ducking under the podium, the only damage, a lost cufflink. He popped his head back up and said, "Damn!" right into the microphone. "My best cufflinks. Where am I gonna find a match?" He held the cuff, cursing under his breath. He'd never said a foul word in public before, and now it was "Damn." How many points would that cost him at the polls? At least it hadn't been "Goddamn."

Donaldson leaned into Reed and whispered. "Every network's got a bead on you. Say something to capitalize on this."

Reed regained his composure. He looked into the cameras and smiled. "We're Americans! Strong, compassionate, loyal. We need to help those who need help, especially at Christmas. And, like Christ, who would have been a Republican if he had the choice, I'm going to forgive this poor, wretched soul who just took a crack at me."

The crowd looked disinterested.

"Not only that, I'm going to give him a job!" There was a smattering of applause as the Secret Service beat the crap out of the sniper and dragged him away. Reed said to Donaldson. "They think I'm fodder for the mill. Just wait."

Donaldson said, "You're gonna give him a job?"

Reed whispered. "Sure. Appoint him Ambassador. To someplace that has lots and lots of land mines. And I mean lots. And have them plant a few. Oh, and those Secret Servicemen—pull their Christmas bonuses."

17

Donaldson said, "Gotcha."

At this point, the little mouths on the worms were opening and closing, yelling, "Tree! Tree! Tree!"

Reed smiled again into the cameras. "Well, fellow Americans, there's only one thing left to say. Merry—"

Reed pulled the switch on the Christmas tree. The electricity wrapped its way up the tree, lighting each bulb in a spiral pattern all the way up to the large angel on top. That's when something went wrong. The switch shot a thunderbolt that locked Reed's arm like a shackle. Reed struggled against the light, but the energy traveled around the frame of his body, making an unnatural glow, like a human sparkler. Then, announcing their demise with a loud pop – pop – pop, the pretty little bulbs on the tree exploded one by one, traveling back down the same spiral pattern. Sparks shot from the angel's ears. Reed's mouth was open like he was trying to speak but no words emerged, then he was blasted into the crowd, a 185-pound cannonball.

Donaldson stood there for a second, his tense jaw dangling open. Finally, he said, "Start the choir." The choir started singing, "It's Beginning to Look a Lot Like Christmas." Mrs. Reed tried to spot her husband in the crowd. "I hope he's all right. I had a watch engraved for him, and I can't return it!"

Reed had blasted through the worms and landed on the lawn. He'd knocked a few people over and was slumped in a heap. No one helped him, the crowd just stared in shock. He was no longer sparking up, but steam wafted from his singed flesh. Donaldson grabbed a Secret Service man. "Get an ambulance!" The Secret Service agent never looked him in the eye. "Impossible in this crowd."

"A helicopter."

"We could do that," the Secret Service man said, then nodded to the tree. "But that pine-scented monster could spark up and kill us all."

Donaldson stamped his feet. "Do something!"

Santa snapped the reins and rode off in a large sleigh pulled by eight tiny reindeer. A catatonic President Reed was propped up in the back of the sled, a small teddy bear tucked in his arm. Donaldson sat next to Reed, grabbing the back of his suit when the bumps jostled him. Donaldson spoke on his walkie talkie, but no one was on the other end, and he mumbled aimless directions as the sleigh rode through the snow. Mrs. Reed sat next to Santa and waved to the crowd like she was in the Macy's Day Parade. "Merry Christmas!" she called. "Merry Christmas!"

At the edge of the White House lawn, Junior came running out, closely followed by Chet. He yelled, "Santa, Santa! Come back!"

Despite the crowd, the Secret Service, the fire trucks that had been called out in case of a flare up, and the labyrinth of empty hoses, Junior wriggled through the chaos and ran after the sled.

"Come back! Please! Come back! Santa, it's me! Junior! Junior Worthy! Remember last year? I left you a whole bag of Chips Ahoy! Okay, so I ate a couple, but gee whiz!" The sled rode away, and Junior collapsed in the snow.

Chet ran over to Junior who stayed in the snow. "He's gone, Chetsky. And I didn't get to give him my list!" Then something cracked inside, and Junior started kicking and screaming, a full-blown tantrum. "Gone! Never pays any attention to me! He's just like my father! I hate Santa!"

Junior stayed parked in the snow but called in the direction of the sled that was long gone. "And that year I wanted the surfboard! You brought me shoes. Shoes! Whaddya know about gifts! Shoes? You crazy, fat, loafer! They were ugly shoes, too! They looked like something my mom would buy. Hippie! Get a shave! Get a real job!"

By this time, Caroline had spotted Junior and ran over. She spoke to Chet. "He didn't bite you, did he?"

"I learned my lesson last time," Chet said.

Caroline crossed her arms and looked at Junior in the snow. "Get up." Junior didn't stand up, but he did sit up, his butt parked in the white flurry. He was sad, wearing a miserable clown frown, and he said, "Hello, dear."

Caroline said, "Where have you been?"

Junior stood up. "I got snow in my pants."

"I don't care if you got snow in your pants or anywhere else. You just missed the most important night of your career."

Junior's sad look morphed to shocked disappointment. "They were going to let me light the Christmas tree?"

Caroline bit on her lip again, then said, "Reed got electrocuted."

Chet's mouth made a little "O," emphasized by his trimmed mustache. "Let's talk voltage, ma'am. Are we talking Everready battery? Or are we talking Hoover Dam?"

Caroline said, "We're talking snap, crackle, dead."

"Oooh! I'm gonna have to record that!" Chet said.

Caroline continued, "We may not have to suffer through two more conventions."

Chet added, "And I may get to be Secretary of State after all."

Junior was trying to dig the snow out of his pants. He looked at them and asked, "What are you guys talking about?" Caroline said, "If Reed dies, you're number one."

Junior whispered, "I get to be president?"

"Yes!" Caroline said.

Junior jumped up and down, then did a backflip like a little windup monkey. "I get to be president! I get to be president! Yippee!" Caroline and Chet grabbed Junior and gave him the eye to shut up.

Junior spoke softly, "I get to be president! I always wanted to be president. I mean, I really, Really, REALLY want to be president!"

Caroline said, "Let's cross our fingers and hope Reed kicks the bucket."

Junior crossed his eight fingers.

Chet said, "Damn. My good black suit's at the cleaners."

Chapter 3

The mood in the room was somber. Donaldson sat in a stiff chair. He was rocking forward, but only slightly, and his right leg quivered nervously as he kept an eagle stare on Reed. Mrs. Reed sat next to the bed and held John's hand. President Reed, a mountain of energy only hours before was now hooked up to a half dozen machines that buzzed, popped, and whirred. A doctor and two nurses hovered over him. The doctor examined the charts for a second time, then gave his pronouncement.

"That was a close one, but it looks like he's gonna make it."

The weight on Donaldson's shoulders relaxed. His leg stopped shaking. He inhaled fully through his nose and was able to take a complete breath. *Safe!* he thought. Mrs. Reed was babbling away to John, saying how she knew he would be okay, how he would be home soon, how this would be the best Christmas ever. Donaldson knew one thing—he needed some sleep. The hospital chair would do. Reed was out of the woods, but it would be best if he stayed close by his side.

That's when Junior, Chet, and Caroline ran in.

Junior said, "How's he doing, Jim? I mean, do I get to be president?"

Donaldson gave Junior a dirty look. The doctor spoke. "He's on a respirator. But if he pulls through tonight, he'll make it. And that's looking pretty good."

"Ah, crud!" Junior said.

Donaldson said, "Go home, you sniveling chunk of bat guano!" He gave Junior a good shove, sending him flying into the wall.

Junior smacked into the plaster then slid down the wall into a heap. "Good thing I'm already in a hospital." He dragged himself along the floor, blurry and unstable. Donaldson wanted to smack him again, but John was more important.

"Well, that's good news," Caroline said, and it was obvious from her tone that it wasn't good news at all.

"Yes," Donaldson said. "Everything's under control now. We all should head home and get a good night's sleep."

"Shouldn't Junior be in charge? Temporarily, I mean, while the president's unable to fulfill his duties," asked Chet.

"No worries. John's at the top of his form, ready to handle anything." As Donaldson spoke, a long line of drool rolled out of Reed's mouth.

Junior still groveled along the floor. He reached up to find anything to help pull himself up. He grabbed wires and pulled, and as he stood, the plugs popped from the backs of the machines.

The tone from the heart monitor changed from blip to bleeeep. President Reed's vital signs began to fail.

The nurse was shocked. "We're losing him."

The doctor said, "Damn! He'd just stabilized!"

Junior stumbled from the machines. "Maybe I wasn't ready. Oh well. There's always five years from now. And six too."

The nurse monitored Reed's vitals. "Pulse is down. Breathing irregular."

Junior continued his reverie. "I guess it just wasn't my time."

Donaldson freaked. He grabbed Reed and shook him. "Dammit, John! You've got to pull through!"

Mrs. Reed added. "Think about the watch, honey."

Donaldson grabbed the doctor by the stethoscope and pulled him over. "You've got to save him! He's our only hope of winning next year!"

The doc looked at him and said, "Dammit, Jim! I'm a doctor, not a politician!"

The EKG flatlined. The machines stopped. The small group stood watching as it happened, it was panic and pandemonium, as if they were running in full circles at full speed around the room, while in reality, they all stood frozen at attention. The monotone howl wailed in the lonely night, illuminated by fluorescent bulbs. President Reed was dead.

The doctor bowed his head. "He's gone."

Junior looked at the doc like he was nuts. "He's not gone. He's right there. God, no wonder the president died. That guy needs glasses."

Donaldson looked to the ceiling, as if an answer for the future was coded in the dots of the acoustic tiles. "He's expired. And with him goes the last gasp of my career."

Junior held up the wires he had yanked out. "Hey, I screwed up the air conditioner!" Everyone looked at the plugs. Then at each other. Then at Reed.

Donaldson couldn't believe it. The dumb motherfucker had done him in. He had told Reed to dump him, but Reed had waited one holiday too many. Now what should he do? His first thought was to find a laundry chute and shove Junior in, face first. "You'll have to wait till tomorrow to be sworn in," Donaldson said, poker faced, his voice masking his true feelings.

Junior really didn't know one way or the other. "All right. Can I wear a sweater? What about a Pittsburgh Steelers jacket? Or do I have to wear a tie?"

"He can be sworn in right now. As a matter of fact, he has to be sworn in," Caroline said.

"Technically, we can wait till tomorrow," Donaldson said.

"Technically, nothing! I want a Supreme Court Justice in here NOW!"

"You know, none of this is going to fare well with the American people. When they find out Reed was rallying when your husband brought him down."

"It's not like he murdered him," said Caroline.

"As a matter of fact, in most states, it is like he murdered him."

"I know what you're up to, and it's not going to work."

Caroline and Donaldson exchanged evil eyes. He stared her down, then shifted, looking away then up. She gave him the deep freeze and wouldn't break her gaze or even blink. Donaldson could feel the tense pull of her bottom lip. She heard his teeth grind.

"You know, um...." Chet looked from Caroline to Jim, ready to mediate. "Um... nothing."

"That's what I thought," Caroline said. She tossed the sheet over Reed. Then tugged her purse from the floor and walked out of the room.

Junior and company were quickly shuttled to a cloistered business office in the hospital. Supreme Court Justice Costa prepared to swear Junior into office. "Wowee! I get to be president!" Junior opened his jacket and kissed his medal, the indigo heart. The medal was the only connection he had with his real father, and Junior wore it every day. He'd been adopted by Fletcher Worthy, his real father's army buddy. Junior whispered to the medal, "Do you hear that, Dad? I get to be president!"

A military photographer raised his camera to record this moment for history. A glazed Mrs. Reed stood nearby. "Raise your right hand," Costa said.

After a moment of thought, Junior said, "Left hand, wedding ring!" A sheepish grin curled on his lips.

The justice said, "Repeat after me—I do solemnly swear that I will faithfully execute the office of the President of the United States."

"Execute? Cool! All those hours of playing 'DOOM' will finally pay off!"

The Justice said, "You need to state the oath."

Junior followed, "I do slalom." He laughed. "And I do slalom. I'm a kick-ass slalomer. Y'know, I cross country, too!"

Costa said, "The oath, please."

"Boy, that's an awful lot of words, do I have to say them all?"

Caroline gave him a swift karate chop right between the shoulder blades. That's when the photographer captured history. Junior rubbed his back.

"Ow! C'mon, hon, you don't have to hit me. It's not like it's our wedding."

The justice tried to hold his temper. "I do solemnly swear that I will faithfully execute the office of the President of the United States."

Junior held his hand up again and said, "Ditto!"

The justice continued, "And will, to the best of my ability, preserve, protect, and defend the Constitution of the United States."

Junior said, "Whel-lup! I'm sure gonna give it the old Worthy try!"

Donaldson turned to Mrs. Reed. "And with that, our worst nightmares have come true."

Junior, Caroline and Chet left quickly, but Donaldson and Mrs. Reed walked slowly. Donaldson continued. "I told him right before he announced his running mate that here was this small possibility that he might die in office. And was Junior the kind of person we wanted running the country. I wish he'd listened to me!" Donaldson shouted to the heavens. "Well, what do you think now, John?"

Mrs. Reed smiled and stared at Donaldson. "Why, Jim, where is John?" Donaldson rolled his eyes and tugged Mrs. Reed along with him as he left the hospital.

As he arranged the press conference, all Donaldson could think was, *not much of a Christmas present*. It was early morning, and the coffee had been fresh and strong, just like every day. But there wasn't enough caffeine in all of Brazil to brace him for this day's hell. The press had been kept at bay and were eager to get the official word on Reed's fate.

Donaldson walked into the briefing room. He recognized all the faces. He'd seen the same people almost every day for the past three years. But this morning, they just seemed a mass of eyes, noses, and mouths smeared together in a blurry human stew.

One person yelled, "Where is he?"

Another yelled, "How's the president doing?"

A third, "Is he okay?"

Another, "Did he pull through?"

The voices were spinning around like a tilt-o-whirl, merging into a common voice that resonated like a snapped bass string, humming its sorrowful tune through the empty air, *"You're through. You're finished. You're outta here, chump."* All the years of building, the sucking up, the ladder-climbing, were deflating like a child's balloon that had been pricked... and, in this case, the prick was one J. "Junior" Worthy.

Donaldson's military training had prepped him for crises. He looked straight ahead, remembered he was an American, and began. "Last night at approximately 9 PM Eastern Standard Time, the president was electrocuted in a mishap instigated by the National Christmas Tree. He was taken to Bethesda Medical Center where he was revived." What the hell was he talking about? Even he didn't know.

He heard the murmurs among the press, like piranhas, sharpening row after row of their little pointy teeth.

He continued. "Due to complications, at 11:20 PM Eastern time, The president was pronounced dead. Vice President J. Junior Worthy was sworn in at that time. I'll take a few questions."

The first press spoke. He knew her face... what was her name? "Mr. Donaldson, did the president have any final words?"

Donaldson, "Yes. He said, 'And to all a good night.'"

Another press person spoke, another name he should know and went blank. "How's the First Lady holding up?"

"The First Lady is a strong human being. An admirable American. One we should all respect. She took four valium and a shot of bourbon and called it a night."

Without being acknowledged, another person spoke. "I'd like to ask the vice president a few questions."

Junior was facing the wrong direction. A few aides turned him around. He faced the mic. "Shoot. Ooh, bad choice of words." Junior looked at the room. He'd been there plenty of times before, but now everything looked different, like it was a completely new world. The light seemed brighter, the people seemed closer, the sounds were louder. He had stepped into a new land.

The press person forged on. "Mr. Vice President, were you with the president when he died?"

Junior said, "Yes, as a matter of fact, I—"

Donaldson cut off that particular question. As much as he would like to see Junior hanging on a skewer for pulling the plug, he knew better than to use this venue for justice. He flattened his tie, repositioning it under his suit. "Next question."

Another press said, "Vice President Worthy—"

Junior held out his index finger. "It's President Worthy, now."

The press continued. "President Junior, your SAT scores were in the double digits, yet somehow you attended Yale. You were allowed into Law School through the EOP, though there seems to be no category that you would qualify under, you graduated last in your class.... you passed the bar on your eighth try, and there's some evidence that someone took it for you. And as vice president you haven't done a single thing right. There are a considerable number of people who feel you're, well, not intellectually rigorous enough to be president. How do you respond?"

Junior said, "What's that supposed to mean?"

"Some people think you're too dumb to be president."

Junior looked at him. "I don't care how stupid I am! I can run this country as well as the next guy!"

The press said, "So what's your first plan as president?"

Junior checked his notes, then said, "The first thing I'm going to do is get organized! And I'm going to start that by... does anybody see page two? Anybody? Do you see page two?" An aide casually slipped a hand to the floor and picked up the page Junior had dropped and handed it to him. Junior rustled through the two pages of his prepared speech. "And then we're..." He thought he found his spot, but he hadn't. He folded the speech and put it in his pocket. He said, "Okay, for starters, now that I'm no longer the national joke, I've decided to declare the national joke the 'knock, knock'." He braced himself for his first real act as president, then continued, "Knock, knock?"

No one responded. The uneasy feeling of a cricket chirping in the remote woods was felt.

Junior was upset. "C'mon guys, knock, knock!"

The entire press corps hesitated momentarily then reluctantly, and almost in unison asked, "Who's there?"

Junior said, "The president. Get it? Me! The president." He cracked up and continued laughing for far too long. The Press corps seemed to be in a state of shock. Junior was on a roll. "In honor of our national joke, I will start every speech with a knock knock. I've got the country's best speech writers working on a couple of zingers right now."

The first press who had spoken said, "Omigod, it's worse than I ever thought."

Another added, "You said it. We are gonna have a field day!"

A third popped up and took a picture with a large flash while another press member added, "He's a gold mine!"

Junior said, "Are there any other questions? I mean ones I can answer."

The press clamored, all raising their hands and calling, "Mr. President! Mr. President!"

Someone who hadn't spoken yet asked, "Hey, Mr. President! What branch of the service was Colonel Sanders in?"

The second press person said, "Mr. President! What's the capitol of Washington D.C.?"

Another who had previously been silent asked, "Mr. President, how many Democrats does it take to screw in a light bulb?"

The Democrats were getting to screw in light bulbs? Man, he could barely get his wife to do it at all! He hadn't heard about the light bulb thing. Maybe they were even having orgies... how did they fit all those Democrats into those little light bulbs? Maybe it was one of those long fluorescent tubes. Dang it, this was a mess. All his life, he'd wanted to have the press calling his name and asking him questions, and now they were doing that, and he didn't know what to say. He looked around, then picked one.

"Okay," he said, "you first."

"Mr. Vice President, I mean, Mr. President, what's your greatest priority? And what course of action will you take?"

Junior said, "Um, my priority... and all of... our priority... and the course we'll take, of course, is the er... uh..."

Chet signaled from the wings. He rocked an imaginary baby in his arms. Junior said, "The priority is a tiny little boat on a rough sea." Chet shook his head NO! He tried again, rocking the baby even harder. Junior said, "No... It's a really big boat?" Chet held up someone's kid and waved the kid around. Junior said, "Our priority is conga line dancing." Chet rocked the kid in his arms. Junior said, "Ah yes, my priority, and yours too. It's the future. The youth of America. That's it."

Chet nodded, then collapsed.

Junior said, "Whew! We've got to turn the current trend among youths around. Youths. Young people. In the common vernacular—kids. Right now, kids have to choose between violence and drugs and gangs and... and... and dammit, there need to be more options. So, I have a plan to get our young kids off the streets."

Junior drew an indecipherable sketch on a nearby whiteboard then said, "Hopscotch. It's not just a girl's game anymore.

Chapter 4

Not on his face, but deep inside, Donaldson smiled. He didn't need to do a damn thing. The press would reveal Junior to be the jackass he was, then Junior would resign, or someone competent would be offered up for the election, and soon things would be back to the lovely status quo. Then again, it couldn't hurt for Donaldson to speed up the process. After all, it would happen anyway. He was just a catalyst. And like any good reagent, he would remain immersed but invisible. Junior, easy. Chet, a breeze. The only possible threat to any plan would be that conniving bitch, Caroline.

Reed lay in state in the rotunda where he was smothered with Christmas crap— Santa bears, candy canes, even some twinkle lights like the ones that had apparently done him in. Then the funeral came, and he was buried in Arlington. Reed's flag draped coffin was lowered into the grave as Junior gave a few final words.

He said, "He lived tall like a Reed, he was cut down like a Reed, and now he's being buried like the proud Reed he was."

Mrs. Reed asked Donaldson, "What the hell is he talking about?"

Donaldson said, "I haven't a clue."

Junior went down on one knee and tried to sing to "My Way." "And now, the time has come, 'cuz he faced, the final curtain. They're lowering the crate, they're gonna shovel dirt in.... Parody, folks. No copyright issue."

The Military post gave the first rounds of a twenty-one-gun salute. Junior grabbed his chest and said, "Oh you got me! He opened his coat and showed he was only kidding. He said, "Hah! Kidding!"

Donaldson leaned to Mrs. Reed and whispered, "He wouldn't be so lucky if I was behind that rifle."

Even before the last croissant sandwich was chugged down at the wake, Mrs. Reed was a footnote to history. They packed up her clothes and her knickknacks, her pictures, her books—they even sedated Wags with a puppy tranquilizer—and tossed everything into a modest black van. Donaldson watched from the window as the van slowly pulled away. An aide escorted Mrs. Reed down the hall. "I really don't need to go shopping, honey. I want to lie down." Too drugged up to realize this was the end of the road for her, the aide escorted her out the door and into the nondescript Lincoln Town Car.

Would the hatchet come crashing down on his neck just as quickly and unceremoniously? He needed help. The number wasn't in his cell. No, this was the type of information one only kept on paper. Evidence that could be physically destroyed to be certain it was gone for good. He popped up the smoky lid of his rolodex and flipped through the worn cards. His middle finger stopped on one. *Pizza Pi.* He hesitated. He could feel his blood pressure go up, up, up, point after point. Well, he certainly couldn't do it himself. He tucked the card in his pocket and headed out to try and find a desk phone. It was time to place a specialty order. And after placing his request for a special delivery, there would be no turning back.

In the Oval Office, Junior was hammering the fourth nail into the wall, chunks of plaster and ruined nails littered the floor. The fourth nail went in straight and stayed. "Hah!" He framed the nail between his two hands like it was the Mona Lisa. He picked up a dartboard and hung it on the nail. He stepped back and admired his handiwork, then moved the board a bit to the right. He picked up a dart and hurled it, full force. The dart landed in the wall, half a foot away from the board. He tossed another. It went through the open window. "Vice president. What a lousy job. I don't know how I ever let them talk me into it."

Chet inched away as far as possible from the darts. He said, "Your daddy told you to do it."

Junior said, "Now Tip Murphy can be vice president. Let's see how he feels when everybody makes fun of him."

Chet said, "I'm sure he'll get a big laugh out of it."

"I am going to be the best president ever! Everyone's going to love me! Chetaroo... you're my best friend. Let's make a pact to always be best friends and never, never fight or squeal on one another. Deal?"

Chet was always reluctant to enter any pact with Junior. Previous pacts had cost him the nail on his big toe, his Louis Vuitton keychain, and most of the paint on the left fender of his Camry. "Well..."

"I'll make you Secretary of State."

Chet said, "Deal." He knew he'd end up getting dragged into the pact. He may as well get something out of it. They rubbed two fingers across their tongues then slapped the two fingers with each other, they tapped each other's elbows and thumped each other's forehead with the heel of their hands.

"Friends forever, it's a deal, never fight and never squeal."

Four blocks away at the local waterhole, The Ballot Box, Tip Murphy picked up his second drink. He liked scotch. Good scotch. And as far as he was concerned, any scotch was good scotch, and his favorite brand was more. He was a big man with a red, puffy face and unkempt hair. His best friend/lawyer/girlfriend, Wanda Castillo, tossed back a highball.

Murphy looked glum. "Hurrah. If it's such a great opportunity, why does it include J. Junior Worthy?"

Wanda said, "Vice president. The number two job."

"Great. Vice president to the biggest joke in the book." Tip circled his finger on the rim of his glass then kicked back the last of the scotch.

She said, "How bad can it be?"

"Being associated with that numbskull is career suicide! I may as well swallow my revolver right now."

"So quit."

Murphy shook his head. "And won't that look great. Abandon my country in its greatest hour of need." With the flag of his finger, Tip ordered another round.

Wanda polished off her drink. "Whaddya know. Life stinks."

Murphy rolled the ice cubes around in his empty glass. "Then there's the press. When they're done dragging the skeletons out of my closet, it'll look like Halloween. If it's illegal, I've done it. Fraud, embezzlement, everything shy of murder..."

"What about that time you were with the Chicago Bulls?"

"Well, I was drunk and don't remember much of that, but one of them sent me a dozen roses. I'd like to believe it was Michael. Or maybe Dennis Rodman. And like I've said a million times, it wasn't a gay thing. More like an initiation... or a rite. It was a one-time thing. Maybe it was the booze." For a moment, he was lost in a reverie. "Michael, Michael, Michael." Then he snapped out of it. "But oh, those halcyon days are gone! Junior's vice president! It's like being named Vice Captain of the Titanic. This country's gone from being great—a place where you could get away with almost any crime—to having a joke for a president."

"Well, Tip, you got that right. This country's gone from being great to being a joke. And it can't even be a good joke, it has to be a knock- knock. It's enough to make you sick."

A strange new look appeared on Murphy's face. A look Wanda had never seen before. "Wanda, that's it!"

"What?"

"What if I WANTED to do my best as vice president—I wanted to serve my country—I wanted to make this all work for the good of the people—but I couldn't because I was sick."

"You just had a checkup!"

"I'm not really sick, you ninny! His idiocy's already rubbing off on you. I'd just say I was sick. To get out of it and keep looking good. This is fucking brilliant! It has to be something that no one can prove."

An eyebrow raised, the roll of her eyes and shake of her head said Wanda wasn't buying it. "Why can't you just tell the truth?"

"The truth?" Tip said as he reached for the fresh scotch that had just arrived. "The truth never got me anywhere."

The buzz of the booze hadn't quite worn off, but the press conference would happen with him or without him. A handful of press corps, totally bored, were all but slumped in their seats. One loudly clipped his nails. One played Tetris on her phone. Two or three dozed off. Junior tried to build a cat's cradle.

Junior said, "Then if you grab it here and here, it's cat's cradle. Hurry, hurry, lookit! Rats!" He bungled the cat's cradle and was left with a ball of knotted yarn more like a cat's coffin. Jim Donaldson had a shit eatin' grin on his face, and he smiled full on at Chet. Junior said, "Oh well, I guess I won't show you my new yoyo trick. Instead, now I'd like to introduce our new vice president.

Speaker of the House, Tip Murphy. If I get shot, at least you can say I left a big Tip!"

Murphy stood at the podium. He glanced at Wanda who stood in the wings. She gave just a slight shake of her head showing she thought it was wrong, wrong, wrong.

Murphy was sure Junior didn't know a single name of these fabulous press people. But he knew them all. Sam, Anne, Taylor. How many times had he fantasized this day? How many times had he practiced this in front of a full-length mirror, casually selecting the right person, aiming his index finger at him just as if the scenario had never crossed his mind. Practiced, calculated casualness. Folksy. Friendly. That's how he'd be when he got his chance, yeah, totally laid-back, as if he'd been doing these pressers for decades. How many years had he waited for his chance to shine, and now here he was, organ grinder to a spastic monkey.

Murphy cleared his throat. "Thank you, ladies and gentlemen. I am deeply saddened by the loss of our dear President Reed. It gives me great honor to serve as our nation's vice president... I only hope that you'll accept me for who I am."

From their deep hibernation, the press started to stir. Though a green cube dropped into a row to complete it, Anne looked up from her cellphone and missed the next block on Tetris. She said, "Huh?"

Murphy plowed on. "You see, I have an illness. Well, it's not a physical illness. It's a psychological disorder."

Sam jumped out of his seat. "Where's my tape recorder?"

"In my current position, I've been able to control myself. I only hope to God I can keep it up. So, if you'll allow me, I'll do my best to serve as vice president. As long as my illness doesn't interfere with the task... or national security... or the safety of any of the staff...."

Anne said, "What is it?"

Sam yelled, "Are you manic-depressive?"

Murphy paused, and it was all for drama. He looked to the podium. He tried to make a tear well up in his eye. Dammit, why hadn't he brought the onion for his handkerchief? Too late for tears, he faced the crowd with a red, puffy puppy dog frown. "Oh, if only it was so simple. You see, I suffer from MPD. That's right. Multiple Personality Disorder. I'm sure you've seen it on "Oprah." That's where I first learned of my condition. And if you want me to resign my position, let's just say no hard feelings."

The Press were alive. They jumped up, waving their hands. Flashbulbs started popping. The room came to life, pumping, pulsing. The fervor and sweat made Tip flashback to his first erection.

Taylor waved, "Tip, how many personalities do you have?"

He hadn't thought it through. He hadn't expected questions. He figured he'd make the statement, they'd ask him to resign, and that would be that, call it a day. No questions. Casual. Laid back. So, it wasn't ending a world-wide crisis, it wasn't solving domestic angst, it wasn't a declaration for freedom, but dammit, it was attention! Murphy cleared his throat then spoke. "Uh... sixteen men, three women... and a Rottweiler. Be careful—when you make me mad, the Rottweiler comes out. Remember—you've been warned."

Anne said, "What's the Rottweiler's name, Tip?"

"His name, is uh... Fang."

Junior and Caroline stood to the side, amazed that Murphy had stolen the show. Junior looked at Caroline, "Oh great. It's just like when I was vice president. I'm getting upstaged by a dog."

Junior was shocked back into the press conference by the bark of the angry dog. When he looked up, he saw Murphy growling and barking into the mic. *Damn!* He thought. Why couldn't he have barked into the mic instead of the cat's cradle? People love dogs more than cat's cradles!

Murphy continued, "I told you. Don't get me riled up. I haven't had my shots." Everyone laughed. There was a sparkle in Anne's eyes. A sparkle! He had cracked the steel curtain. In an instant he felt it, and the sparkle confirmed it—he was a media darling! Oh joy!

"Who are the females?"

Murphy said, "They're separate from me, the reality is, I don't always know when they might—" Murphy swooned at the mic and it looked as if he would fall into the podium. The press gasped, then Murphy blinked rapidly and spoke in a Southern accent. "How-dee-doo, y'all. Oh, I'm Blanche and I'm here to tell you, I don't want reality. I want magic! Yes, yes, yes, magic. Magic. I don't tell the truth. I tell what ought to be the truth." The press broke into applause. Murphy, as Blanche, waved a royal hand of thanks.

Caroline shoved Junior. "Get in there and be a leader. Take control."

Junior looked like a whipped pup, scared back to his kennel by Fang. "How?"

Caroline pursed her lips and stared at Murphy. "Look at him. He's stealing the whole show! Why couldn't YOU have had multiple personalities?"

"Give me a chance! I'm still working on one!"

Murphy was having a field day. He was making love to that mic like an old man who had just downed a month's prescription of Viagra. Off to the side, Wanda wore a look of concern.

Murphy now spoke in a female voice. "I'm Zelda."

Sam winked. "You're kind of cute."

Murphy continued in his Zelda voice. "Think so?"

Sam said, "I do."

Murphy continued in his bad falsetto, "Good, cause I'm a radical feminist ready to bust your cajones."

The press clamored to Tip. Press people waved microphones, notepads, pens, and they pushed into the podium. Instead of forty voices, there was now one. "Mr. Vice President! Mr. Vice President!" The forty press people merged into one gorgeous voice, and Tip was joyfully swallowed up into the lovely sound, recklessly spinning into the beautiful swirl of the press and photographers.

Chapter 5

The next day, Junior sat at the breakfast nook, munching on cereal and reading the Washington Post. Caroline drank black coffee and dreamed of toast without ever indulging. Five-year-old Jeffrey Worthy also ate cereal. Junior put down the Post and poured a second bowl of Fruit Loops. There was no joy in Mudville this morn.

"I don't know why I have such bad luck." Junior poured milk into his breakfast bowl until it overflowed all over the table. "Oh no! What is it, Caroline? I try so hard to do everything right."

She looked at him. "It's just the way you are, Junior."

"As a matter of fact, anytime I actually try and do some work, things seem to backfire even more. Why? Why, son?"

Jeffrey stopped eating his cereal and shrugged. "I don't know."

"Well, I want you to think about it. And see if you can come up with an answer."

"Okay, Daddy."

The first family dog, an Irish Setter trotted up to the table and rested his head on Junior's thigh. Junior said, "You too, Red!" Junior tossed the paper in front of Caroline. "Look at these headlines!" He started reading them aloud.

"*22 Vice Presidents for the Price of One.* And this – *We Flip for Tip!* And this one makes me want to puke. *We Love You, Mr. Vice President.* Murphy scores big time and I'm a big-time flop."

Caroline said, "Don't read and eat at the same time. You know it's too much for you."

"He gets to go on Geraldo, 'n' I have to go to the budget meeting. Boring! Hey, who took the prize out of the Fruit Loops?"

Caroline bit her lip. "You did, dear."

"Oh," He said. "I want this job more than anything! I'll make the people of this country love me! Hey, do you think if I said I had a brain tumor or something, they'd love me?"

Inside at the budget meeting, the frustrated members of the Budget Committee sat around the table.

Congressman Dexter said, "Where is he?"

Congressman Nighthorse said, "Who knows?"

Another piped in, "Maybe he was struck by lightning!"

"Dreamer."

Dexter said, "We can't conduct this meeting without him."

"He's already forty minutes late. We need to have this meeting with him. We should reschedule it," said Congressman Chavez.

Just as he said it, Junior entered. "Hurrah, I'm here! Sorry I'm a little late. I wanted to see what the 'Today Show' had to say about me. Hey, where are the donuts?" Junior scoped out the table for something to eat. He found nothing, so he opened his briefcase.

Congressman Chavez said, "Finally we'll get down to work."

Junior, "When I became president, I really thought the snacks would be better. I get hungry. Low blood sugar. Luckily, Caroline packed me some Zingers. I just love the raspberry!" Dexter cringed as Junior wrestled to open the plastic wrap. Was it the intolerable crunching of the plastic or the ineptitude of Junior's fine motor skills? Hadn't Zingers been discontinued years ago? Dexter snatched the package from Junior's hands and tore it open with one pull.

"Thanks!" Junior said. He munched on his raspberry Zinger, sucking the leftovers off his fingers with each bite.

"So, who here thinks I'll be the greatest president ever? Don't be shy, raise your hand. And what about this crazy budget? Do you think we'll be able to buy a new car, or will we have to ride on the old wheels another year?"

Dexter chaired the committee. He came from big business, and he made no other allegiance. He had been a thumbnail away from getting the Social Security reform pushed through and now he had to worry about this new administration. It wouldn't be hard, not with Junior's track record, but still, there was that worry—what if it didn't pass? *Don't count your chickens*, he thought. Dexter smiled at Junior, then spoke. "Our priority, of course, is Social Security. And, collectively, we feel we should cut Medicare by eight percent to balance our current budget."

Senator Weinstein was a progressive from California. She always wore a red suit and had a helmet of hair, impeccably coiffed. She was sixty-three and looked every minute of it. She said, "That is the most fiscally irresponsible recommendation I've ever heard. That type of fiduciary reduction will result in long term—"

Senator Douglas Kim piped in "—Of course you want to cut the programs that will affect the elderly and the poor." Senator Kim was Korean American, and he always fought for the little guy of any cultural background. This was Kim's second term in the Senate, and he knew Dexter still thought he was Chinese and couldn't get it through his head that Kim was born and raised in the United States and that English was his only language. Whenever Dexter didn't like Kim's point of view, he would repeat what he said at the top of his lungs, as if Kim didn't understand him.

Senator Dexter paused. He looked over his reading glasses. He hated the bitch from California and the annoying Chinese guy. It didn't matter though, he had an ace so far up his sleeve, he could bet his whole pot. Dexter nodded his head like he gave a shit what the two commie senators thought, then, with the most innocent of his looks, he asked, "What's YOUR feeling on this, Mr. President?"

Junior looked around and behind him. "Umm. This is a very complicated issue. But, uh, it all sounds good to me."

Weinstein said, "But what do you think we should do?"

Junior played with the last bite of the Zinger. "Well... Caroline usually handles our cash."

Kim said, "You must have some experience administering a budget."

Junior said, "Actually, none. So many numbers!"

Kim tried not to let his voice reveal what he was really thinking. "I see. How did you get this far?"

Junior knew the answer to this. "Sheer personality! Tell you what. You boys... and girl... figure out the number part, and I'll come back and affix the old J. Junior Hancock. Howzthat sound?"

Dexter said, "I like it."

Wilson piped in, "Works for me."

Douglas Kim didn't like it. "President Worthy, you are abdicating your duty as president."

Junior was shocked. "Abdi-what? Man! Do you talk to your mother with that mouth? You boys really need to clean up the foul language in this room. Besides, I'm not... what you said... I'm just not gonna do it. That's all. I've got something more important to do."

Weinstein said, "Mr. President, what could be more important than our nation's budget? Than protecting the elderly? Than Social Security?"

Junior said, "Well, uh.... Golf."

Weinstein said, "Golf?"

Junior said, "Yeah. Now that I'm Prez, I gotta practice. I'd hate for someone to beat me. I gotta hit the links!" Junior started to leave. "If it's okay with you, I may send Caroline by to sign that thing for me."

Kim said, "Mr. President, it is not okay."

Dexter yelled at Kim, "HE'S GOING TO AUTHORIZE HIS APPROVAL!"

Kim always stuck to the book. "Mr. President, forging your signature is improper... I'd prefer to use the word, illegal, but I won't. I'll just say it's irregular."

Junior said, "Irregular? What's signing that thing got to do with dropping a deuce? Anyhoo... Caroline does it for me all the time. Sign for me, I mean. Not drop a deuce. She's backed up worse than an LA cloverleaf. Anyway, let her sign! Don't worry about it. And you know what they say—Five!"

Kim mouthed in an unsure way "five?" Junior poked the Kim in the stomach. "That's fore! Plus a hole in one! Hah! Gotcha, Dougy, you dog."

Junior left the boring meeting and walked down the hallway. He was doing sort of a Kevin Bacon dance from *Footloose* as he traveled, and, from the end of the hall, he saw his Dad, Congressman J. Fletcher Worthy.

"Hi, Dad!"

Though the only time he'd ever been on a horse was for a photo shoot, Fletcher Worthy always wore boots and a cowboy hat. He said, "That's my boy! The President."

"Yeah. I did it."

"You did good, boy. You were in the right place at the right time... that's all I've ever expected of you, and you lived up to it."

Junior beamed. "Thanks, Dad."

Fletcher Worthy reached in his pocket and pulled out a scratch of paper. "Now, I've got a list of things you're gonna be changing... just little things, like laws and requirements."

"Oh, do I have to? I wanted to play golf."

"Golf? I was supposed to be at a health care meeting. What the hell! I think it's time for a little father-son bondage! I'll meet you at the club, boy."

"You're on! Dad, Dad, I'll bet you a can of soda, wait, wait—I'm the President—I betcha a can of beer I beat you on the greens!"

Fletcher raced off to get his clubs as Chet came running down the hall. "Junior, what are you doing here! You're supposed to be in the budget meeting!"

"Oh that—dang, Chet, it was hella boring! Anyway, I already went."

"It's over?" asked Chet.

"Don't worry Chetaroonie. I took care of everything. Now here's a list of changes we're gonna make." Junior handed his Dad's list to Chet. Chet skimmed it and was horrified.

"This is totally illegal! You can't do any of these things!"

"But, Chet! My Dad said I had to!"

"Junior, it's against the law."

"Chet. What's more important? The nation's law... or your Daddy's law? Know what I mean?" Junior slapped Chet on the back. "I know you'll take care of it, Chet, you're a champ!"

Junior continued down the hall. From nowhere, Jim Donaldson appeared and walked alongside him. Junior entered the study, and Donaldson followed. Donaldson stared with a deep, laser-like glare, as if he was cutting Junior for abdominal surgery. "So, how's it going?"

"Being President's terrific. I should've applied for this job a long time ago. Today, I'm going golfing, and this time, *I'M* gonna drive the cart."

"Golfing. Wasn't there a budget meeting?"

"I handled that already. This President thing is a breeze," Junior said.

"Oh," Donaldson said. "I just wanted to say, if there's anything you need, you can trust me."

"Really?"

"Yes."

"Well, right now I need my golf clubs." Junior ducked his head in the closet. "It's not like a pair of glasses—they're here somewhere."

57

Donaldson was unsure if he should look for the clubs, but right then, Chet entered carrying the clubs.Chet gave Donaldson the same look one give's a guy who's horned in on their girl. "Here are your clubs. You left them in your old office."

Junior grabbed a nine iron. "Terrific!"

Chet gave Donaldson the look a second time.

"Well, I guess I'll be going," Donaldson said, and he walked out the door.

Chet shook his head in disgust. "You can't trust that guy."

Junior looked at Chet, shocked. "He just told me I could!

Chapter 6

The studio was packed. Tip eyeballed the crowd. "Where's Geraldo?" he asked the producer.

"Sorry. Geraldo decided this was just too tacky. He sent his friend." Right then a nondescript white guy with a mustache and a blue suit appeared. He spoke in the mike.

"Tonight, on a special 'Rivera Reports,' who put the vice in the Vice President? I'm Geraldo's friend."

The audience applauded wildly. While Geraldo had done his best to transition back to serious newsman, his friend was ready to serve as tabloid ringmaster. And this audience was a circus—it included New Yorker natives, tacky tourists, and selected individuals with MPD. When they saw the camera was on them, they went through multiple transformations. Some audience members carried signs reading "We love you, Tip! (all of you!)" and "Multiple personalities are better than none!"

"Tonight, we'll take a look at the fascinating world of multiple personalities. But this is no grocery store clerk, no dreary housewife, this is our very own Vice President, and he's joining us to reveal the very essence of his true self." Geraldo's friend took his seat on the stage next to Murphy. "So, Tip, I hear you're an arsonist."

"Well, Geraldo's friend, I'm not an arsonist. That's Rod. I like to call him Lightning Rod."

Geraldo's friend passed the mic to a member of the audience. "I just want to say that I'm an arsonist too. I was responsible for the Palmdale fire and the Allen Heights blaze, and I just want to say, Rod, you're an inspiration to us all, and I'm behind you all the way."

"Tip, do you think you could pull up Rod for us?" Behind Geraldo's friend, a cop handcuffed the audience arsonist and hauled him away.

"It's really not something I have control over."

Suddenly, the smile on Murphy's face froze, it curled into a snarl, the upper left lip pulling up until bared teeth gleamed into the lens. First one eye, then the other, rolled back into their sockets, and when they dropped back into place, they were on fire.

Murphy swooned, and his tongue jutted past his lips, the veins on his neck popped out, and the rather large Murphy pulled his flab around to a point that he almost appeared lithe. Murphy had transformed. He had traveled down the River Styx, spawned upstream, and returned as Lightning Rod.

In his Rod voice, Murphy said, "Hey, Geraldo's friend, why's your mustache crooked?"

Geraldo's friend covered his mustache.

"It's not!"

"Sure it is. A rich guy like you ought to be able to pay somebody to even out your mustache!" Murphy flicked Geraldo friend's mustache.

Geraldo's friend was pissed. "I pay good money to have this mustache trimmed!"

Rod said, "Why don't you save your money and put it where it'll do you some good—like a gym membership, Fatty!"

Geraldo's friend dropped his journalistic skills and shifted to talk show jerk. "Watch it, punk! I box. I'm in terrific shape! I do cardio. And I box. And I will punch you right off this stage! Because I box." He turned to the cameras to deliver his next line. "I just want to say that guys like you are the worst scum on earth."

"Back off, loser, or I'll set that lip fuzz on fire." Murphy pulled out a lighter, held it up, flicked it on, and cackled. The audience went nuts. Forget foreign policy, domestic crises, terrorism. This is what they had come to see. Wanda, watching from the wings, rolled her eyes and shook her head. The audience was berserk with enthusiasm. "Rod! Rod! Rod! Rod!" The audience embraced their inner mob and chanted with glee. Murphy kept flicking the lighter on and off. The mob would scream and jump and holler. It was what he had always wanted. He had them! He owned them! He had them in the palm of his hand, and all he needed to do was to trip the flame!

Fletcher and Junior were out on the links. Secret Service Agents followed them on foot and in carts. Reporters and cameras tagged along, hoping Junior would at the very least ricochet a ball off an innocent spectator. Junior said, "I still don't see why I can't drive the cart. I mean, I'm the *President.*"

Fletcher said, "You're still my kid."

Junior said, "I still think I should've been a pro-golfer. I would've been a helluva pro-golfer. And then I could get to do commercials and have big, fat endorsement contracts. Just like Tiger Woods. I woulda been Tiger Worthy. Don't you think I should've been a pro-golfer?"

"Junior."

"Yeah?"

"Shut up."

"Okay. The Press are here, Dad. Why do you think that is? What are they looking at me for? Oh! It's like I AM a pro-golfer. Hey, Dad, pull over. Let's listen."

Fletcher was never one to hide his feelings about the press. He cleared his throat and spat. He said. "When are you gonna learn that the press are nothin' but a herd of piranhas? It's a good thing you're adopted because I'd hate to think that fouled brain of yours is genetic."

"Well, maybe the piranhas would like to see me putt. Say, Dad, how is it that if I'm adopted, my name is Junior?"

"It's because I love you, boy."

"Oh, okay. That makes sense."

Junior got out of the cart and grabbed his putter. He whispered in his soft golf announcer voice, "Tiger Worthy steps up to the shot."

One of the press said, "Mr. President, aren't you supposed to be at the budget meeting? That's what it says on your daily agenda."

Junior said, "No, I'm supposed to be golfing."

The second press said, "What's your stand on the proposed cuts to Medicare and Social Security?"

Junior spoke softly from the side of his mouth, "What's my stand, Dad?"

Fletcher always knew the right answers. "Well, you're for what the people want."

Junior faced the press and smiled. "I'm for what the people want." The second press member asked a follow-up. "What do they want?" Junior started mumbling. "What do they want... you got me there." Junior lined up the putt, took a swing, and ate a chunk of turf. The patch of sod flew through the air and smacked his Dad in the shoulder. Two more shots, and he'd made his putt. Junior and Dad got back in the cart. There was half a minute of silence, then Junior spoke. "Boy, they expect you to know everything! Pull out the Presidential cellular. Get me the Press Secretary—the Secretary of Press?"

Fletcher said, "I thought he was your Secretary of State."

"Whatever he is—you know—Chet!"

An aide pulled out a cellular phone and handed it to Junior.

"Chet? President Junior here... I've been thinking. No, really. No, it wasn't daydreaming. Daydreaming has pictures. I was just thinking, Wow! I'm the President! And it looks like this president job could actually turn into a bit of work. And I'm not going to flub this up. I'm willing to do whatever it takes! So, I want you to set me up with a bunch of really high-profile appearances all over the place. I'm going to learn how to do this. And I'm going to be the best President ever!"

Geraldo's friend's shirtsleeve was badly torn. He addressed the camera. "Welcome back. This has been an extraordinary show. We've seen twelve of Vice President, Tip Murphy's, twenty-two personalities, including the young boy, Mikey, the Southern belle, Blanche, and the Rottweiler, Fang, who as you can see, ripped up my sleeve and urinated on my pant leg."

One audience member stood up and said, "I just want to say God Bless You, I wish you the best, and I know you'll be a great Vice President." The audience applauded.

"Thank you, thank you," Tip said, as Tip.

Geraldo's friend handed the mic to a young girl. The girl had stringy, dirty blonde hair, wore smudged glasses, and had a crooked mouth that wasn't helped by her need of braces. The girl said, "Mr. Vice President, I have MPD too. I quit going to school because the other kids made fun of me. But because you've made this disease okay, I'm no longer embarrassed, and I've decided to try and go back to school with the other kids. Thank you, Mr. Vice President!"

Murphy was now Blanche and spoke precisely, with a Southern accent. "Everyone deserves a fine education, so I commend you, young lady! I am proud to serve as your Vice President, and I want you to hold on to one thing! Always remember, despite our personal weaknesses, you must never give up—after all, tomorrow is another day."

The audience went wild, applauding until their hands were raw. Murphy stood up, invoking the spirit of the last scene in Gone With the Wind, he held his fist toward the heavens like Scarlett O'Hara clawing her way back to Tara, and he said it again, "Tomorrow is another day!" The crowd didn't care that she was blurring different fictional characters. They gobbled it up like a calorie-free chocolate mousse. People jumped from their seats and ran to the stage, grabbing at Murphy's clothes, shaking his hand, slapping his back, hoping his Midas touch would transfer just one measly iota of Tip's magnetism.

From the side of the stage, Geraldo's friend was wrapping up. "Thank you, Mr. Vice President. This has been an enlightening and educational hour. We'll see you next time on Rivera Reports." As they closed, Murphy barked and howled and bared his teeth at Geraldo's friend who quivered, dropped the mic, then ran out of the studio.

Chapter 7

The shadows, the false illumination of the fluorescent lights, the potential for a stalker to grab a person by ankles and take them down, these lovely elements make all parking garages seem ominous, but they're oh so much worse at night. Boogeymen lurk behind the hubcaps, and new urban legends hide in every trunk. Donaldson curled through the paranoid darkness. He spotted his contact... at least he thought he did. Donaldson gave the agreed signal then moved into the light, a fluorescent with one side flickering. His contact hovered in the shadows, not showing his face, leaning, with only his back in view. All Donaldson could see was one big ass butt.

Donaldson said, "Long Dong?"

The butt in the dark said, "Long Dong's sick. I'm Fat Ass."

"You know what I want?"

Fat Ass hissed the answer. "Yesssssssss."

Donaldson said, "You know why?"

Fat Ass said, "I can guess."

Donaldson said, "Are you going to do the job?"

"That depends."

Donaldson said, "Well, it's got to be clean. On my end, I mean. There can't be anything to trace it back to me. That would defeat the entire purpose."

Fat Ass said, "I understand."

Donaldson tried to get a glimpse of the face of this giant human ass, but no luck. "There it is then. We'll meet again. Soon."

Fat Ass wasn't finished. "One question."

Donaldson gave a nod of the head, indicating it was okay to ask. The Ass said, "That electric Christmas Tree and Reed... was that you?" Donaldson's poker face drew no card and walked away.

Caroline Worthy loved clothes. In the Vice-Presidential quarters, Caroline had a large walk-in closet. She had lots and lots of clothes—off-white skirts, cream colored sweaters, mocha suits. She had played her cards right. She had appeared as the dutiful, conservative wife. She had worn beige, fawn, mushroom, camel, sand, and taupe. When they moved from the Vice-Presidential

68

quarters to the White House, she ordered all her clothes destroyed. She had wanted them burned in a bonfire, but they just threw them in the trash. She didn't need to play the Stepford Wife anymore, oh no. She had wanted the cherry on the top of the sundae, and, damnit, she'd gotten it. She was the First Lady, not the Second Lady, the First Frickin' Lady! She didn't need anyone's approval, she no longer needed to be on guard. Now she could show the world her true Beauregard style... yes, it wasn't Worthy style, was it? And it never would be. It was Beauregard style. If only her mother was here to see her triumphant coronation.

She said, "All these years... and finally, my dream has come true. Now I can run the country. Too bad Junior had to come with the bargain." She stepped into the gown. Her hose slid against the satin liner, and she pulled it up. Dawn, her assistant, zipped it. Caroline had thought it would need to be fitted, but the dress was snug, the fabric pulled tightly across her hips. The dress was a tower of brilliant purple sequins. A floor length gown with a slit to the thigh. Caroline looked at herself in the mirror. *This*, this was who she truly was—a stunning brunette—Dorothy Lamour, for god's sake! She needed to adjust her lipstick—more pouty. And more lift, more body to the hair. A bustier would pump up her silhouette. This was it. From now on, she would live her life in full color. Chartreuse, fuchsia and gold. Purple sequins were king. Beige was dead. Long live purple sequins!

Donaldson walked in and was nearly blinded by the shiny flecks. He crouched then started edging around her. "What are you doing?" she asked.

"If you stand still, I can comb my hair." He stopped. "You wanted to see me?"

"Yes," Caroline said, trying to force a purr in her voice.

"To show me your Charo imitation? Needs more class, less leg."

"It's time we bring dignity back to the office of the Presidency."

Donaldson said, "I couldn't agree with you more."

"If that's some sort of comment on the competency of my husband..."

"I'd never be one to say your husband is incompetent. And I'm the first to admit his wife is more than competent."

"My husband's asked me to tell you something."

"What?"

"He'd like to thank you for your service. He's found a replacement."

"He's firing me?"

"No."

"Oh, so you're firing me? Well, isn't that just dandy."

"It's not personal. It's politics."

"I could help him."

70

"You and I both know he's better off without you."

"Who's the replacement?"

"Chet."

"I thought he wanted to be Secretary of State."

Caroline ignored him. Donaldson left, unable to make a dramatic exit—the wall-to-wall carpeting kept him from angrily clicking his heels, and he didn't shut the door as he left, so he couldn't have the moment of angry closure he'd hoped for.

"He's gone," Dawn said, then she placed a tiara on Caroline's head. Caroline checked herself out in an ornate mirror. She said, "Mirror, mirror on the wall, who's the most feared of them all? Yes, I know!" She cackled, out of control.

That Chet was a real go-getter. He had arranged a speaking engagement immediately, one where Junior could show he was a top-notch President. Junior had known Chet would do right, but he never thought he'd get such a great gig! He was speaking at the National Mime Convention. He was gonna have to get that Chet a raise—a big one. Now, this was an audience. Classy. Everyone came formal, almost everyone wore a black coat and a black and white striped t-shirt. Oh yeah, and everyone wore a hat—they were formal, these Mimes—and most had white face makeup and bright red lips. Even the people who weren't white wore white makeup. The place looked like a family reunion—of mimes! Several held big flowers or wore fancy boutonnières. Junior took a deep breath, but he was inhaling more than air, he was sucking in the pride of a nation as he ended his speech. "In closing, I'd like to say, a mime is a terrible thing to waste."

The National Mime Convention was abuzz with silence. All the mimes mimed applause, except one who pretended to eat the table centerpiece. Junior pulled an imaginary rope and left the stage to the mimes' rousing inaudible applause. Success! He had done it! He was a hit!

The moment of triumph had ended, and it was time to head home. Junior, Chet, and Caroline walked along near the Lincoln monument. Junior held his arms up in the air. "Thanks for joining me on this little walk of all I own. Whaddya know? I'm a smash! This President gig is going to be a breeze!"

He pointed at the Lincoln Memorial.

"Look, there's the guy on the ten-dollar bill!" He ran up to the monument. "Someday, they'll build a statue of me and put me on some money." He stretched his arms and shouted. "I'm the President! I'm the President! I'm the President!" Just as Junior was flapping his wings, Congressman Butts walked by. "Oh, hello, Congressman

Butts, from the state of Illinoise. What're you doing up so late?"

Butts said, "I was working."

Junior said, "Working? Since the daytime?"

Butts said, "Doing this job right takes a lot of time."

Junior said, "Guess what, tonight I spoke at Clown College, and I was funny!"

Butts said, "That's good. Now you just need to work a little harder."

Junior said, "And if I do, will people like me?"

Butts said, "Being President doesn't always mean people are going to like you."

This was not what Junior wanted to hear. "But if they don't like me, I won't get re-elected! And if I don't get re-elected... I won't be the President anymore. And I really, really, REALLY want to be President."

Butts said, "Junior, being President isn't just about being liked. It's about leading the country. Having a vision. Inspiring the people."

Junior said, "Shaking their hands isn't enough?"

Butts had a smile and a little chuckle. "I'm afraid not."

"But the jokes! They liked me!"

Butts said, "You need to be more than liked. You need to listen to the people. You need to know their hearts. Then you've got to do what's right. Taking leadership may mean making decisions that aren't popular, but if the people trust you and you've thought things out, then you can be successful."

Junior said, "Yes, but can I get re-elected?"

Butts said, "Just remember, Jerry, being President means putting the happiness of the people before your own."

Junior said, "Boy, that wasn't in the job description!"

"I'm sure you'll find plenty of things that weren't in the job description. I have. People are suffering, and you're in a position to help them."

"Okay," said Junior. "I want to help them."

Butts started to leave, then stopped. He looked back at Junior, looked into his eyes, shining brown pools of innocence. "Junior, I have something for you."

"You do?"

"Yes. It's a gift."

"Cool."

With care, Butts pulled out the pocket watch. He wiped his thumb where the etching had worn away. It was the watch he had hoped to give to his son. But there was no son. Bessie's only pregnancy had been stillborn. A baby boy they'd named Randall. They had tried several more years with no success. The watch would have gone to Randall. Butts had grown more

Congressmen and women than any U.S. politician. He had influenced several prominent African Americans, and he had mentored people from all races. Maybe, somehow, he could help this fledgling leader. Maybe this young man, unprepared for the service that fate had dropped in his lap, could transform into a compassionate leader.

Butts took the watch from his pocket. It was the timepiece that had watched the world change, watched his career grow, watched his life progress. Butts popped it open, a gesture he'd done for the past fifty years, knowing this was the last time he would open the watch. "The day I passed the bar, my mother gave me this watch. It cost her every dime she had. She told me to remember how swift the time passes on this planet. And that time waits for no man. A reminder to spend every minute wisely so when I passed on, I would know I stood for justice, I had served the people. My time will soon run out. Now it's time for you to take the baton." Butts pressed the watch in Junior's hand and gave his hand a squeeze.

"Oh, I've already got a watch."

Butts smiled. "I want you to have it anyway."

Junior shrugged and put the watch in his pocket. "Okay. Thanks."

Caroline had been watching the whole conversation take place and she just couldn't take anymore. First, she was shocked Butts had called him Jerry, since no one ever used the J. of J. Junior. Second, to think Junior could actually do anything of value, do anything right, do anything at all! That was a hoot. And since when had a U.S. President been a real leader? "Excuse me, Congressman."

Congressman said, "Yes, Mrs. Worthy?"

Caroline shooed Junior away. "Junior, why don't you go clean Lincoln's fingernails." Junior walked toward the marble Abe. Caroline looked at Butts. "I don't think you understand. Junior won't be much of a President. He won't be much of a leader. He can't be. He doesn't have the capacity. And we all accept that. You should too and get what you can out of it while you can."

Butts replied, "I am not interested in what I can get. I am interested in serving my country... and her citizens."

Caroline's voice was so sarcastic that the cement she stood on buckled. "Right!"

Butts nodded his head. "Good evening, Mrs. President." He walked away.

"What an idiot," Caroline said.

Junior dangled from Lincoln's hand, his feet doing the cha-cha in the air.

"Honey, I've done my best, but we really need a professional manicurist in here! Y'know, what this guy really needs is a shave."

Junior hoisted himself up, then balanced upside down. He rubbed Lincoln's beard with the soles of his shoes. It was almost like riding a bicycle. He pushed hard with his right foot and felt something give... probably a curl of the beard.

"I'll get rid of this five o'clock shadow in no time—WHOA!" Junior kicked his right foot and felt a break, but it wasn't his leg that had broken. He must've hit a weak point in the marble, and a slow, cracking sound started, low at first, like a large tree falling in the distance. "Wuh-oh!" Junior tried to make it better by pushing one more time with his foot, one more push would make it even. That's when the small cracking sound turned into a deep earthquake rumble. The statue trembled, and Junior fell into Lincoln's lap. He looked up and saw Lincoln's head crack off, then bounce off the knee, just missing Junior. Junior watched Lincoln's head roll away. It bounced down the steps, missing two, then hitting the third, careening down the walkway until it disintegrated at the bottom of the steps. Once the head of Lincoln, now a billion bits of dust.

Junior had a Cheerio of a mouth on. "Whoopsy!"

Caroline said, "Are you okay, dear?"

Junior said, "Yes."

Caroline said, "Damn."

Junior said, "Good thing nobody saw."

Near the water, hidden in the darkness, Fat Ass zoomed in with his video camera, recording Junior on the headless Lincoln. Junior jumped down and assumed a stately pose on top of the rubble that was once Lincoln's head. Drilling holes in the neck and planting the dynamite caps without being seen had been a son of a bitch, but he knew before the week was out Junior couldn't resist climbing on Lincoln.

Junior said, "Four scores and seven yards to go, our nation brought forth the great game called football!"

Junior, Chet, and Caroline look at the headless Lincoln monument. Junior said, "Maybe no one will notice. We can just say some terrorists did it."

Chapter 8

Donaldson shut the door, sealing himself off from the world, just the way he liked it. He walked across the hardwood floor, each clip of each step echoing through the hall, and every echo resonating in his gut, asking if he'd wasted his life.

Well, had he? He turned that question off. It really didn't matter. This was where he was at right now, and he couldn't control or change things that had already happened. There was, however, one thing he could control. One thing he could change. Junior Worthy as President. His cell rang. He had relaxed about the landline and decided the cellphone was safe enough. "Pizza Pi? Is my order ready?"

"Sorry, no delivery tonight."

"I see. Are you short delivery boys or did you run out of ingredients?"

"The delivery happened. Just like you ordered it—all the ingredients. But the yeast. It just didn't rise."

Donaldson hung up the phone. Worthy was a dummling. They were much harder to kill as their aimless nature made escape easier for them. The idiot had survived the first attempt. He would have to get all the details from Fat Ass, but oh, the irony, the symbolism of Abe Lincoln's head rolling off and pulverizing the fool into dust. But the nincompoop had survived. Maybe Donaldson could wait it out. Just let it happen, let the people take him down—it was inevitable, but so damn slow.

Donaldson looked through the freezer. He should've gone out to eat. He selected one of the frozen dinners—beef tips with Portobello mushrooms. He put it in the microwave, the light was the only glow in the kitchen, the hum of the microwave the only sound. He wouldn't be suffering through one more frozen dinner if Reed was still alive. No, he'd be sitting in the formal dining room, eating a world-class meal.

He had been fired. And not even by that little wiener of a loser. By his wife. His *wife*. That bitch. Waiting was not an option. Letting it happen was not good enough. It would have to happen on demand. His demand. Fat Ass was already a part of it. Revenge. It was the American Way. Plus, that stupid little SOB had killed John, maybe not his best friend, but definitely his best ally. He owed it to John.

Caroline had changed into a teal, silk nightgown. She wore a matching robe, belted tightly at her waist. Junior entered, still wearing a suit and tie. He narrowed his eyes at her then ran his tongue along his lower lip. Caroline stared at him. Junior slipped his jacket off, spun it around, then let it fly, like a two-buck stripper. He loosened his tie, then pulled one end, trying to seductively let the tie fly as well. Instead it stuck in a knot, and Junior fell to the ground, struggling, strangling himself on his tie and unable to get it off. He finally stopped, wheedled the knot out, and pulled the tie off. He stood up again and buffed his butt with the tie, pulling it left, right, left... left, right, left. Caroline crossed her legs. Junior pulled off his shirt, shoes, and pants and started dancing around in his underpants and t-shirt. This was his "love" dance. Caroline had watched it almost every night for twenty years.

He landed on the bed and puckered up to Caroline. She didn't kiss him. "Daddy wants to play." Caroline picked up the remote and turned on the TV. She said, "You have two hands... use them!"

"I want to be with you!"

"Junior, I've told you, you get your birthday and Christmas. That's it."

"But I'm the President!"

"I don't care if you're Alice in Wonderland. I'm not messing up my hair just so you can *relax.*"

"Rats! What's the point of being President if I can't even bump the fuzzies!"

Chet explained, "It's sort of an impromptu press conference, but we have to address this. Just read the teleprompter." Chet ushered Junior into the Press room, and the questions started before he could even read a statement. Everyone was shouting, "Mr. President!" And he could hear them saying there had been security cameras but they had all been disabled. Chet parked him at the podium, and he started to read off the teleprompter.

"Ladies and gentlemen, the destruction last night of one our country's most iconic symbols, the statue of Abraham Lincoln, is unprecedented and unforgivable." Luckily, the words had been spelled out phonetically. "We're going to find who did this, and we're going to persecute them to the full extent of the law."

"Prosecute!" Chet said.

"That too," said Junior. He picked up on the teleprompter again. "This is abominable. Abominable? Like the Abominable Snowman?" That teleprompter was like trying to win the 3rd grade spelling bee. Impossible. Junior gave up on the teleprompter. "Well, whatever. We're going to fix Abe Lincoln's head, and I don't just mean a duct tape job. Where he got— you know..." Junior dragged his finger across his throat with a cutting sound. "But until we do, I'm ordering we place a giant, cardboard smiley face as a substitute."

It was early. Donaldson had grabbed a cup of coffee, and the hot cup in his hand was comforting. Donaldson slipped a badge to Fat Ass. He still couldn't get a good glimpse of him, but he hadn't needed to know what he looked like just to steal someone else's ID.

"The entourage is scheduled to pass in front of the Ashton Building at 10:10 AM. The press has already reported there'll be sharpshooters positioned on roofs throughout the city. Junior will be sitting in the back, passenger side, though it won't break my heart if you take out his wife too." A thought that had never popped into Donaldson's brain now landed— "You ARE a sharpshooter, right?"

"I've been firing a weapon since I was eight."

That wasn't the question, but Donaldson was sure Fat Ass could handle it. He watched as Fat Ass assembled his rifle. "I thought you were pulling in reinforcements for this."

"Lincoln should have ended this. He didn't. Now it's personal. I wanna take this motherfucker out all by my lonely."

Donaldson sat at an outdoor table, casually drinking another cup of coffee. It was already 10 AM. Where was he? The roof was empty. Where was he? The Beast rolled down Brookings Avenue, police escort, Secret Service in tow. Donaldson watched the fat Cadillac slowly roll right in front of the Ashton building, turn right, and it was gone. Just like that, it was gone, and so was the chance to blow Junior's head off.

Was Fat Ass just going to walk off with his money? Then he saw it. It looked like a hand. Yes, it was a chubby hand, struggling for a grip. Grappling, struggling, then finally securing and hoisting. Finally, a small head popped over the edge of the building. Then, slowly, the head was shadowed by the giant buttocks. Like a sunrise, the humps rose, until they stood, proudly poised at high noon. Finally, the barrel of the rifle appeared. It scanned the horizon, then came to rest. Even from the café, Donaldson was sure he could hear the burdened breathing. Damn that Fat Ass!

Murphy was in Junior's office. Though he'd dreaded working with Junior, the truth was much worse than anything he could've imagined. Junior had called him in for a

84

strategy meeting, and before he knew it, Junior was riding Murphy like a pony all around the Oval Office. Chet stood on the desk, horrified, but impotent. Junior was talking in some sort of insane singsong babble, "I'm the president, I'm the president, Ride 'em, Mr. President."

Murphy wasn't sure what would crack first—his temper or his spine. Finally, he couldn't take another second of it. He started to roll Junior off his back, and as he did, he pulled back his right and let it fly. The bare fist landed square on, a direct hit to Junior's jaw. Murphy could feel the ringing in his knuckles. Junior's face froze and, though it took effort, he looked even more dazed than usual.

Murphy jumped up, tried to help Junior to a chair.

Junior said, "Whaaa happen?"

"Oh, sorry, Junior. That was Rod!"

Chet was dumb, but he wasn't stupid. He was still miffed that he wasn't named Secretary of State. He would take Press Secretary, but he wanted Secretary of State. Junior promised him. It would come in time. For now, Chet knew the hopes of re-election were slip sliding away, so he'd assembled a PR team that might have that one chance in hell of salvaging the campaign. Junior and Chet sat around the board table with the eight members of the team. It was headed by a woman in her thirties, cut from corporate cloth, willing to lie, cheat, or steal, and ready to hawk her product, whether it was soda, deodorant, or the new, improved President. She spoke, "Okay, Mr. President, we've come up with a completely new profile for you."

Junior said, "You mean what I'm doing isn't good enough?"

Those at the table exchanged glances. The PR woman jumped in. "As part of the campaign, we want to create a fearless, competent leader."

Another team member spoke under his breath. "Do we ever."

The PR Woman continued. "The big problem is you don't relate to the people. Forty-six percent consider you a spoiled rich kid."

Junior smiled proudly then whispered to Chet, "That means sixty-four percent don't!"

The PR woman pushed forward. "So, what we're after here is a man who is sensitive, nurturing, yet strong and intelligent."

Junior said, "Wow, that sounds great! I'd vote for him. Who is he?"

"So, we'll be developing some commercials to reflect the type of President the American people want. Of course, we'll need to shoot some film showing you doing those things, Mr. President, because we, uh, currently have no footage, of uh, those things."

Junior said, "Sounds like I'm going to be a movie star! This is great! I'll be all Presidential and people will vote for me. Perfect."

"Our first thought, you, on the National Mall, overseeing the repairs on the Lincoln Memorial?"

Chet twitched. "I don't know if that's a good idea."

Junior said, "Nobody cares about Lincoln. That press conference was nearly empty!"

She continued, "Okay, our research also indicates the American people want to see you in action. We want to hold a town hall meeting, interact with the people. Show them you're on their side."

Chet balked at that. "I don't think that's such a good idea."

Junior said, "Why, Chet? I thought I was on their side!"

Donaldson lifted a dictionary. He placed it in a box. He felt his Adam's apple almost bounce against his throat. He swallowed. It wasn't panic. Was it anxiety? Grief? Who was he kidding? He was pissed off. Donaldson and his assistant, Webb, packed up Donaldson's desk. He said, "We've got to find some way to eighty-six this clown so we can get our jobs back."

Webb said, "There's no way in hell they'll run him."

Donaldson said, "Have you ever heard of the GOP not running the incumbent? It's up to us to get rid of him."

Webb said, "If we..."lose" Junior, who will we run?"

Donaldson said, "It doesn't matter. Bozo the Clown could do a better job."

Webb said, "Yeah, and Bozo dresses better, too. Hey, why don't you run?"

Donaldson shook his head then said, "I'm a behind-the-scenes man. I don't fit the mold. Besides, I'm an agnostic, and I'm divorced. Being Press Secretary is just fine with me."

Webb said, "I hear ya. But you're underhanded, you're a liar, and you're willing to kill to get what you want. I think those are the qualifications of a great president."

Donaldson said, "Why thank you, Webb."

The South Lawn had been set up for a welcome ceremony with the Japanese Prime Minister. Donaldson had finished his packing and was taking one last look at the grounds before he left. He sidled up to Chet. "Is he ready for this?"

"I prepped him myself," Chet said.

"Yeah?" Donaldson said. "Shouldn't you be focused on Lincoln's head?

Chet turned to Junior. "This is your chance. This is how we stay in office. The whole country will be judging your ability to handle foreign policy with how you handle this. The trade pact is popular. All you have to do is sign it. Plus, we want to use this footage in your PR campaign."

Junior said, "What are you trying to tell me Chet?"

"Don't blow it."

"Gotcha."

Junior welcomed the Japanese Prime Minister. "I thought you'd be wearing, you know, a kazooki outfit or something. A ninja, or better yet, anime!" The Prime Minister bowed. Junior bent over to see what he was looking at. The Prime Minister bowed again.

Junior yelled as loud as he could, "Did you lose your contact? Contact! Contacky Lensy!!"

Donaldson wrinkled his brow, then leaned into Chet. "Oh, you prepped him to be racist? Interesting choice."

The Prime Minister bowed again. Junior looked down. He checked his fly then snuck a glance at his shoes for dog poop. Junior said, "In honor of this historic meeting, which shows our two great countries can get along, I'd like to present you with some All-American gifts. First, a windbreaker." Caroline held up the windbreaker. On the back, a logo read *All the*

Way with Reed & Worthy. Junior said, "Guess we won't be needing those! Also, a decanter of liquor in the likeness of the only American King, Elvis Presley. And, finally, I'd like to present you with a carton of unfiltered Camels. Remember Joe Camel? He was a cartoon camel! They got rid of him, but he is so cool! He really made me want to smoke!" Junior cracked up. "SMOKE! SMOKEY!" Junior yelled. Junior said, "This language barrier is a bitch! Chetty, next time get me a prime minister who can speak English. Somebody from Britland or something."

The Japanese Prime Minister looked at Chet and said, "Did anybody tell him I speak English?"

Donaldson, "Oh yeah, Chet, did you forget to tell Junior the Prime Minister went to Princeton?"

The Prime Minister said, "Thank you so much. You're very generous. I would like to present you with some traditional Japanese gifts."

Junior whispered to Chet. "Cool. I hope it's Pokeman cards."

The Prime Minister gave Junior a kimono.

Junior said, "Mmmm... what's this?"

"It's a traditional kimono. For your wife. I hope she likes it."

Junior whispered to Chet, "Fat chance of that. She's already got one bathrobe. I gave her another one for her birthday and she threw it in my face." Junior tucked the kimono under his arm. He shouted so the Prime Minister could understand. "I'll give it to her later!" Then he gave Chet a look that said, "I'm trashing this thing as soon as we're outta here."

The prime minister handed Junior a samurai sword and said, "A samurai sword. Offered in peace. That our two countries may continue to work together." Junior grabbed the sword and played junior swashbuckler. "Cool!" With a light slice, he chopped off the prime minister's tie. Then he cracked up. "I saw that on the 'Three Stooges!'"

The Prime Minister took a deep breath. "That was a Hermes tie."

Junior said, "Oh, don't get your kimono all in a bunch, buddy. I'll make it all better. Give him your tie, Chetsky."

Chet was obviously unhappy with the idea, but he started to remove his tie. Chet whispered, "Remember what I said."

Junior realized he must be screwing things up. He needed to make it better. "Okay, well, can I get this guy a hot dog or something? A good old U.S. of A. hot dog? That would cheer him up."

Chet looked at him. "No hot dog."

Junior said, "A hot dog would make up for the tie." Junior slapped the Prime Minister on the back. The Prime Minister was obviously uncomfortable with the touching.

Chet said, "Junior! He's the prime minister of Japan!"

Junior said, "Hey, sorry about the tie. But somebody in your family's probably got a laundry, huh? Somebody must have left a tie behind and that makes it a freebie! These little guys kill me!"

"Wow," said Donaldson. "Next time you prep someone to be a racist, tell him to get his races straight."

The Prime Minister looked at his entourage, and they left.

Chet said, "You had a chance to show people you could be a good President and you blew it. Junior, you've just destroyed fifty years of careful negotiating!" Chet's eye caught the PR cameras and realized Junior had just destroyed his next fifty years too.

Junior called after the Prime Minister. "Yeah well, I got one for you, buster, remember, um.... Remember, um... Dang, I forgot whoever I was supposed to remember! Oh well, it must not have been important." Junior dusted his hands and jacket and turned, facing an outraged mob of Americans. He stood there, mouth agape, then said, "Wuh-oh!"

Chapter 9

It was embarrassing. He'd ordered it all online. And bit by bit, the boxes had arrived. Now he had everything. Screw what Wanda thought! This was his ticket to fame, and he wasn't going to let the ticket sit in a closet, he was going to use it. He picked up the carved silver letter opener that had belonged to his mother and slid it across the packing tape. From the Styrofoam peanuts, he lifted the first item, a black case, tightly wrapped in plastic. With a zip of the letter opener, the case was free. He sat at the table in his kitchen. A bright lamp and mirror moved in here only for this purpose burned a hole in the darkness. How many times had he watched someone do the very same thing? Why hadn't he paid more attention? Of course, that's why.

There were four colors. He selected a silky green then picked up the applicator and softly dusted the shimmery green powder on his eyelid. All of a sudden, the colors in the room looked brighter, and a cold shiver made his spine like Jell-O. He remembered the first time he fell in love... it was that same tingle. He looked in the mirror, covered the painted half of his face, then switched and covered the other. The green eyeshadow made him someone new, someone beautiful. He could be a different person every day, with a different point of view, and if the public didn't like what he said, he could just blame the personality who said it. He picked up the lipstick. It was bright red, the same crimson red he'd heard women call their peers tramps for. He pulled the solid red bulb across his bottom lip, it pulled the lip down at first then it turned the glorious red. He watched it all transform in the mirror. Gawd, he wanted to fuck himself!

He grabbed the next box and opened it. He delicately lifted the lace panties. He had to go to Lane Bryant for his size, but their stuff was just as sexy as Victoria's Secret. He held the panties up to the light. They were black, sheer, and he knew there was a matching bra in the box. He ran his tongue across the panties. Manna. He tore off his own pants and briefs, then slowly pulled the panties up his calves, his thighs, then on his hips. He looked in the mirror.

The elastic leg bands were a little tight, right where his butt met his thigh, and that tightness turned him on. He needed to tuck but wasn't quite sure how to do that. His legs needed to be shaved too. But he looked delicious. He took the bra out and ran his finger along the lace of the top. The bra—brassiere—foundational garment—was also sheer black and oh so sexy. He tried to put it on but couldn't buckle it in the back. Now he knew why they sold those ones that buckle in the front. He buckled the bra then pulled it over his head. The C-cups were mostly flat, except for the bit of man-breast he had. He'd read people used bags of bird seed, but he hadn't picked any up. He shoved cotton balls in the cups, filling them up, then he squeezed the cups hard a few times, feeling himself out. The transformation was complete. He was becoming all woman.

Chet was not happy. Junior nervously stood behind a podium. The town hall crowd was two steps shy of a mob. Junior spoke, "Okay, the economy is kind of on the fritz. And I made a little booboo with the Japanese Prime Minister. I said I was sorry. Geez, can't you give a guy a break?"

A woman in the front said, "What you're proposing is outlawed by the Constitution!"

Junior said, "Consti-what?"

One man couldn't take anymore. He jumped up and grabbed a mic. "Look, the unemployment rate is up ten percent, and you haven't been in office a month! The country's in the worst depression since 1929. The only bill you passed was that thing about hopscotch, and when you signed it, you spelled your name wrong. I've lost my job and so have most of the guys from my office. I can't pay my mortgage. My friends are losing their homes. Nobody's got health insurance. This whole country is desperate. We need work. Now! What do we do?"

Junior said, "Haven't they ever heard of the want ads?" Chet whispered in his ear. "Oh. Craig's List. Or better yet, when I've been out of work, I've just dialed 1-800-DAD."

The woman in the front moved to the guy asking a question and grabbed the mic out of his hand. "Hey, you never finished answering my question. What are you going to do about the American children living in poverty?"

Junior said, "Well they've got to pull themselves up by their beltstraps and, and, and... get dressed!

The crowd was pissed. Chet had wanted to cancel after the fiasco earlier that day. But the PR team pointed out that a cancellation would look bad. They would feed the answers to Junior in an earpiece, there would be no trouble. He could turn around the earlier mess. Just as long as he stuck to the script. Then Chet realized Junior hadn't stuck to the script. He never stuck to the script. He never regurgitated the answers he'd been fed. Okay, just as long as he didn't do anything completely stupid. If he just didn't make things worse, they could get through this.

Junior said, "I just want to take a moment to wax the old philosophical surfboard."

Chet said, "Uh oh."

"Chet, he's not using our feed." The aide pulled off his headphones and looked at Chet.

Chet said, "I know."

The aide said, "Didn't you tell him not to?"

Chet suddenly felt as if he was having an out-of-body experience. "Yes," he said, though it felt as if he was on the ceiling, watching himself answer.

The aide looked like he was about to pee his pants. "He's going off script." Then he went up an octave. "He's going off script!"

Chet said, "I know."

"Didn't you tell him not to?" the aide asked for a second time, but he didn't wait for the answer. He already knew it. He started running around like a chicken on Ecstasy.

Junior said, "Many reports of where this country is at are unsubstortiated. But I'm going to try and clean things up."

An audience member yelled, "How unsubstoriated are they?"

"A whole lot. Let's start with the idea that I'm dumb. How could I be dumb and be president? It doesn't make sense. Now, even though I flunked the fourth grade... twice, and yeah, I spelled my name wrong signing that bill, but I was only off by one letter, despite those little bitty things, I want to be known as the education president."

The audience heckled. One guy yelled, "Hey, how do you spell that?

Junior said, "With a capital J—for Junior. And that capital J stands for another thing—Lifelong learning. All Americans should learn their entire lives. I myself signed up for a correspondence course. And if I complete this home study course, I'll earn this nifty certificate and qualify as a VCR repairman, though most folks have switched to DVD. Even if I don't go into the profession, Caroline and I can save a buck at home, and if I'm gonna balance that budget, I better start somewhere."

An audience member shouted, "You just don't get it!"

Junior said, "Of course I get it. It's stupid, the economy. Oh, and it's like some famous guy said... what was his name?

Doesn't matter, but times were tough, and he said, "We have nothing to fear, but—"

"Your administration!"

The audience cracked up and patted the young heckler on the back.

Junior said, "That wasn't nice."

The Town Hall show was supposed to end with the star footage of the day. The PR team had spliced together what they could and somehow had salvaged about forty seconds that looked decent. The commentators interrupted, "Mr. President, now we'd like to share some recent footage of you in action."

Junior smiled. "Look. Look! It's the movie they made of me! Strong, loyal, compassionate!"

The monitors blinked to life, and instead of the PR tape, Fat Ass's videotape of Junior knocking off Lincoln's head began to roll. It was looped and played Junior saying, "Some terrorists did it, some terrorists did it, we can just say some terrorists did it," again and again and again as Lincoln's head pulverized over and over.

A squat lady jumped up and pointed her finger. "He's the one!"

The unemployed guy was shocked, "He decapitated Abe Lincoln!"

Junior faced the camera with a goofy grin. "Wuh oh! This is gonna cost me some votes!"

A large group of protesters gathered in front of the White House. A Rally Rat shouted on a megaphone. "Do we really want an idiot to be president?"

Someone from the crowd yelled, "We've done it before."

The Rally Rat continued, "We need a government for the people, by the people, and... uh, like poor, headless Abe Lincoln said, Power to the People!" The Rally Rat yelled, "What do we want?" The crowd responded, "Junior out." "When do we want it?" "Now!"

Chet pulled Junior into a meeting room. "You need to see this."

On a small TV, Junior watched a newscaster.

"...which started in the DC area have quickly gained ground throughout the country. Let's go to David Marks in Los Angeles. Dave, can you describe the situation for us?"

A reporter in a suit waved off black, billowing smoke. Fire raged around him. Behind him, people ran, some scared and hysterical, others energized by the destruction. "This scene is typical of the rage that's occurring throughout the country as the people call for the resignation of President Junior Worthy." David ducked as a steel pipe was tossed near his head.

The anchorman said, "Can you give us any idea of the death toll so far?"

David never heard the question. He and the crew started running. "We've got to move—let's go!"

Chet turned the TV off.

Junior said, "Looks like we've got a bit of a problem."

Chet said, "Yes, and I've outlined a course of action."

Junior said, "I don't need action. I'll just go out there and calm 'em down."

"It's not that simple!"

"I'll just apologize for the Abe Lincoln thing, and it'll blow over."

Junior opened the White House door and saw protestors everywhere. He yelled. "Hey, get off my lawn!" The protesters looked over at Junior, trying to decide if it was him. Junior shouted, "What the hell do you think you're doing?"

The Rally Rat yelled back on his megaphone, "We want to run the country!"

Junior yelled, "But you don't know anything about running the country!"

The Rally Rat yelled back, "Neither do you!" The crowd agreed and stormed the White House.

"Wuh uh!" Junior slammed the door and ran back to the conference room. "What do I do? What do I do? Let me look through the handbook." Junior took out the book his

Daddy had made for him. "Oh, here it is—call the national guard. That's a good idea. I'll call the national guard... oh, but I was in the national guard. That means guys like me would show up. And what could they do? Make a beer run?"

Caroline entered and said, "What's going on?"

Junior pointed out the window. He said, "Can you believe it? They want me to quit! How can I stop this?"

Chet ran in and said, "We need our best advisors on this."

Caroline said, "Advisors my cellulite-sucked derriere! We need to BOMB 'em!"

Junior said, "Hey, if I can stop the riots, maybe they'll give me the Nobel Peace Prize. That would be cool. Junior Worthy... winner of the Nobel Peace Prize... why not?"

Chet said, "I don't think anyone's ever been awarded the Nobel Prize for cleaning up a mess they started."

Junior said, "Chetsky... I know how to turn this mess around! Call a press conference!"

"We can't call a press conference! We're under siege!"

Benjamin came in. He was a CNN reporter, and his cameraman followed.

"Benjy! Did you risk life and limb to get in here and share the real story with the American people!"

"No, I was already here. I was taking a dump in the Oval Water Closet."

"Okay, but you can help us turn this around," Junior said.

Benjamin nodded to the cameraman. He fired on the camera and adjusted the lens. Junior spoke, "First, I want to say that I'm really, really sorry about Lincoln's head. It was an accident. And I can be a great president!"

"President Worthy, the riots are out of control, there's civil unrest throughout the nation, what's the answer?

Junior said, "The answer is love."

Benjamin said, "Love?"

Junior said, "That's it—L-U-V. Love! Love will bring us together. That's what's gonna save the nation." He turned to Chet. "Help me out... brother."

Junior started singing, loudly and off-key, no recognizable tune and words jumbled up from several songs. "Love, love it will do something! Why don't you just think of me. Not the other guy, it will keep us together, think of me whenever, some lonely guy starts snoopin' around, putting me down la la la la la la la la la la, you better—stop, because you know I think I love you! Saturday! That's when I'm thinking of you, something or other, you know—it's just love!" He finished the indecipherable 70's mashup and said, "Man, we really need a mirrored ball in here."

Benjamin stared at Worthy. He and the cameraman looked at each other. They tossed down their stuff and ran for it. A few staff members got the same idea and cleared out. The aides looked out the window at the fiery riot in full blaze on the White House Lawn. Junior Worthy brushed some crumbs off his jacket and said, "If I'm gonna keep this job, it looks like I have a little work to do."

Chapter 10

The White House was a shambles. Parts of the dome were burned away. Garbage was littered all over the lawn where Willie Nelson had shown up and held an impromptu concert. Although the crowd had dissipated, Willie continued to sing to a couple of Deadheads who were so drugged out they didn't realize he wasn't Jerry Garcia. Willie sang "On The Road Again" as a girl in tight jeans twitched her hips.

Junior and Chet walked the grounds. Junior said, "What a mess! We're gonna have to get that dome fixed. If elected, my first campaign promise is to get this place cleaned up!"

Chet said, "We just got the word."

Junior said, "You did? Was it the "F" word? I'm still trying to figure that one out."

Chet said, "You're not going to be nominated at the convention."

Junior said, "No, Chet, no. I'm the president!"

Chet said, "I know. And you did your best." They poked their heads through a hole in the fence and looked at the mess. Chet said, "Unfortunately, this is your best. The American people should have known better than to elect a fool."

Junior said, "You said it! Darn that President Reed! He was a real jerk! Now what do we do? I need a miracle, Chet."

Chet said, "I don't know. Want to get an ice cream cone?"

Junior said, "Chet, you're brilliant! That's why I hired you."

Junior, Chet, Fletcher, and Caroline sat around. Newspapers littered the room. Headlines listed Junior's disasters. Junior said, "When am I gonna make another speech?"

Caroline said, "Not for a while, honey."

Junior said, "Why not?"

Chet said, "Your popularity has sunk below sea level."

Junior said, "It could be a short speech."

Chet said, "Junior, they want to impeach you!"

Junior said, "Im-PEACH me? Hah! Why can't they im-PEAR me?"

Fletcher said, "Son, you're already impaired. You're about as popular as a hemorrhoid at a nursing home. About as welcome as deviled egg farts in a crowded elevator."

Junior said, "Nobody likes me? But in high school, I was voted Most Popular."

Chet said, "I'm afraid you won't be making the yearbook polls this year.

Caroline said, "You know what this means. I'll have to hock my crown."

Chet said, "Our chances of being re-elected are about as good as winning The Pillsbury Bake Off."

Junior said, "Hey, what if we make some Alice B. Toklas brownies... then at least the judges might be trippin', and we'd win."

Fletcher said, "The only one trippin' around here is you. The whole nation hates you."

"You're wrong, Daddy! The American people love me! They just forgot for a minute. Somehow, I'm gonna wiggle my way back into the cockles of the American heart. And I'm gonna crawl in the aorta and fester!"

Chet said, "Great. We're dying in the polls, and you want to harden their arteries. You've got to take some sort of action."

Junior said, "I've gotta do something to keep this job! Okay, I know! I'm gonna make 'em like me."

Chet said, "How?"

Junior said, "How?"

Chet said, "How!"

Junior said, "Well, since the weed brownies are out... It's got to be something that appeals to the American sensibilities... something that shows my political savvy... something with flair..."

Chet said, "And what will that be?"

Junior took a philosophical pause, then announced his plan. "Lotto."

What on earth was going on. Hopefully, this would be a short-lived phase. She'd been with him for eight years. She thought they were both getting close to retiring. They could get a condo in Florida, walk on the beach every morning with a steamy cup of coffee. But now it was all falling apart. It wasn't the job. She didn't have an issue with him taking more responsibility, he had wanted to serve the country. It was this crazy masquerade of playing a Southern belle or arsonist or dog. It was silly, it was outrageous, it wasn't helping the country, and people loved it. Where was her future now? She could handle it. As long as it didn't last too long. As long as he dropped the act within a few months and went back to the old Tip. And what if he didn't? What was left for her then? Was she going to retire and move to Florida on her own? Coffee for one?

Maybe she should plan a weekend getaway for them. They could go to Rehoboth, walk on the beach there, get a reset. He could get away from the press and the daily grind. That would get him back to normal. They would have a few drinks and laugh it off. He would figure out some way to explain it all to the press. She would tell him that he could do some real good in this role if he would just focus on his mission and stick with his goals. He could really make a difference. Tomorrow, she would bring up Rehoboth... or somewhere, since right now they would freeze their asses off at the beach. Maybe Florida.

He had done everything right. He had been intelligent, loyal, and moral. Well, mostly moral. And what good had it done him? It was like learning the American Dream was only possible for a handful of people. He was fifty-five, and everything he had invested in—his career, his friends, his skills and savvy—it was all thrown to hell. Junior Worthy was human garbage, and he'd lost his job because of Junior Worthy and been canned by Caroline Worthy.

Doing the right thing had been a bad decision. He would never base another decision on doing the right thing. He would make every decision to benefit himself from here on out. Every decision, every day, and he would work his way back to the top. And after he had made sure Junior Worthy was killed, he would put his aim on Caroline. She needed to suffer. She needed to suffer the way he had suffered. That would make him feel better.

Why was it so hard to kill someone so stupid? You'd think it would be easy. He was dumb, walk in front of a gun, pull the trigger, done. Was there some safety in idiocy? Or was Fat Ass the problem. Was Fat Ass even more stupid than Junior? Could anyone be more stupid than Junior? It had to be that Junior had some sort of protection in his dumbness. Maybe the way to kill him was to think as he thought. It takes a thief to catch a thief... maybe it takes a dumbass to kill a dumbass... he didn't need a Fat Ass, he needed a Dumb Ass. But who could think at so dumb a level? Did he know anyone who had the capacity to operate with such freeform stupidity? He would think about it. There had to be someone.

Caroline. How would he do her in? She always seemed like such a prude... he could force her into a showgirl outfit, have her walk down the showgirl stairs, then unleash a bag of marbles on the steps and watch her bounce down the steps, feathers and rhinestones flying, the giant headdress landing on the stage.

Marbles? Showgirl? Really? Was that the best he could do? He was teaching her how to swim, the American crawl. She was wearing a royal blue, single piece, swimsuit, and he stood behind her, guiding her arms, showing how to do the stroke. She was reluctant, laughing, splashing him, not wanting to get her hair wet. He splashed back, and with that, gained her trust, and he eased her deeper into the pool, and she started to move her arm in the stroke, safe in his arms, that's when he shoved her head down and wouldn't let go. She struggled at first, little bubbles rising to the surface. She tried to fight, desperate to save herself, but her thrashing was limited. He was strong. And soon her body became a deadweight and sank to the bottom.

Pool? It was still winter. And he couldn't do it in an indoor pool. Gun? Too messy, and fine for her husband, but too easy for her. She needed to be humiliated, like he had experienced. But what would humiliate her? Being in her underwear? No, she would like that. For all the prudishness, she had a streak of exhibitionism. What would humiliate her? To be poor. That was it. Yes, to be poor. That would destroy her. She had been a rich little debutante. What could be worse for her than to be broke and have the whole world know it.

It was crazy, but everything he needed, he could get at his local grocery store. Everything but the gasoline. He would have to get that at a gas station, though he could substitute charcoal fluid for the gas.... He checked his list. Glass bottle. He went through the liquor aisle—there were bottles of wine, vodka, different liquors. He put a fifth of scotch in his basket. Any of these would work, but he didn't like the shape of them. He had an aesthetic of what he wanted. A milk bottle. Did they still sell milk in bottles? He hadn't bought milk in over thirty years. He rolled the cart to the milk aisle. There were cartons of non-fat, whole fat, two percent, one percent, lactose free, and on and on.... But they were all cartons. They wouldn't work. Then he saw it. A real, old-fashioned milk bottle. There were only a few, he rolled over to it. Organic raw milk. Well, it's not like he was going to drink it. He lifted it up. He liked the heft of it, it was definitely a solid piece of glass, weighted down with the liquid. Was the glass too thick to break? No, it could break. It would explode. It was perfect. He practiced his hurling motion, hoisting the bottle and moving it like throwing a shotput. It was perfect. He checked the price—the quart was three times the price of a gallon! Were they nuts? It was robbery. It was robbery, and he was getting it anyway. He put the bottle in the cart, handling it like it was gold.

What next? Motor oil. That was in the Households section. He wheeled over. They had 10-30 and 10-40. Would it really make a difference for what he was going to use it for? Probably not, he didn't know enough about it, he just knew the oil would act as a thickener. The 10-40 was all purpose, he put it in the cart.

He wheeled to the kitchen gadgets, they were opposite the cake mixes. Vegetable peelers, steamers, measuring cups. So many gizmos. And there was what he was looking for—a kitchen hand towel. Not a thick terry one, more like canvas. It was red and white checkered. He hadn't considered the picnic look, but he didn't have any choice. It went into the cart.

One last thing. Lighter fluid. Should he use lighter fluid for a real lighter? Did they even sell that anymore? Or should he get charcoal fluid. The charcoal fluid was up front. He put a container in the cart. This was Christmas Day for Rod. Tip rolled the cart to an open register.

The cashier was tired. "Having a barbeque?"

"Huh?" Tip said. Then he realized she was commenting on the cart, not reading his mind that he was thinking of barbequing DC. "Yeah. Yes. A barbeque."

"In the winter?" She asked.

"It's always perfect weather for a barbeque!" They both laughed.

He put the bag in the car, hopped in, and buckled his seat belt. Then he just sat there. Fire. He thought about the attraction for Rod. The flickering of the flame... yellow, red, orange. The smell of the burn. The heat. Tip felt his cheeks turning hot. And the sound. The crackle of the fire. It was alluring. And the smell. Not once the smoke became irritating, but when it first started. The marvelous roast of wood... such a gorgeous, primal smell. It was the smell of power. He wasn't Rod, but he could understand Rod. Maybe spreading gasoline around an abandoned structure then lighting it in some way that he could be up on a hill, watching the flame, without getting hurt, he wouldn't get hurt. The thrill, the flicker inside, the fire inside. He didn't want to hurt anybody. He just wanted that giant, massive, hot, inferno, blazing, licking wall of flame. What was he thinking? He needed to get home.

Chapter 11

The White House Lawn had been transformed. There was a circus atmosphere, and vendors sold cotton candy, corn dogs, and Tip Murphy action figures—with a flip of a switch, he turned into Blanche. A large platform had been erected, complete with a Lotto ball chute. People in the crowd wore cardboard masks of Junior. American flag banners and bunting hung everywhere, it pretty much looked like the 4th of July on LSD.

Fat Ass had been ready. Donaldson walked through the crowd, wearing a paper Junior mask. Fat Ass was in military dress—part of the color guard carrying the US flag. God knew where he found pants that would fit. From twenty feet away, Donaldson could see the threads from the seam beginning to unravel as the thick thighs fought for their freedom.

This had been Fat Ass's idea. Donaldson hoped it worked. He peered through the cut out eyes of the Junior mask, trying to get a good look at Fat Ass, but the flag draped in front of his face. Loudspeakers blared the Star Spangled Banner, and the color guard stepped forward. This was it. Fat Ass had sharpened the point of the flagpole into a spear. Instead of stepping forward to present the colors, he was going to lunge and jut the well-honed point directly into Junior's heart. And that would be that. A fitting end to the young upstart. The guard stepped closer and closer to the oblivious Worthy. Junior was sucking the helium out of a balloon then squeaking out, "I'm the president!" much to the amusement of the crowd.

Then Fat Ass made his move. His rapid, first jerk made the whole podium shake. He pounded the risers and aimed the flag, with its razor tip, at Junior's chest. Donaldson guessed Fat Ass could do the fifty-yard dash in just under two minutes. Junior turned to see what was causing the shaking, and the turn saved him. Fat Ass flew past him and off the stage. The pole planted itself in the lawn and stuck. It was just like a pole vaulter, except Fat Ass didn't exactly vault. More of a splat. Junior leaned from the stage, held out his arm, and sang,

"...and the home of the brave!" Then he yelled, "Play Lotto!"

A young news announcer, Carlos Sandoval, called the shots from the lawn. "In a rather unusual move to win back popular support, the president has decided to randomly select an American citizen to provide him with 'the voice of the people.' Back to you in New York, Jane."

Inside the news studio, Jane manned the anchor desk. "Carlos, how do you interpret this move?"

"Well, Jane, I'd say this time, the president's really lost his marbles."

Jane continued, "Oh, I see the vice president's Southern belle personality, Blanche, has been selected as the president's glamorous sidekick."

Blanche wore a stylish wig and fashionable sequined gown. She posed next to the Lotto chute. Blanche took the mic. "They told me to take a Streetcar named Desire, transfer to one called Cemeteries and ride six blocks and get off. Well, if there's something I'm good at, it's getting off!" The crowd laughed.

Junior said, "Okay, American people, I want to say again I am really, really, super sorry about that Abe Lincoln thing. Honest, I was trying to make things better. Now, welcome to our All-American Lottery! We're gonna start by raffling off this canned ham." Blanche displayed the ham, delicately brushing her manicured nails past the label. "When you came in, you were given a ticket. And now the lovely Tip, I mean the lovely Blanche, will pull the winning number. Blanche."

"Could you please turn down those awful lights! They are harsh beyond a delicate woman's nerves." Blanche reached into a fishbowl and pulled out a ticket. Stretching every vowel for all it was worth, she said, "The winning number is 0034982. Please come claim your ham!" The crowd rustled around, checking out their numbers. Blanche said, "Check your tickets. Your ham is waiting." A goofy looking guy in the crowd, pushed his way through. "That's me. I'm the one. I felt lucky all day. Make way."

The Ham Winner jumped up on stage. He held up his arms in victory. Blanche said, "We have a winner. Step right up, you lucky man." The Ham Winner snatched up the ham then leaned in far too close to Blanche. "Howzabout a kiss, Blanche?" She pulled away, then relented, "Okay, but just one. Don't muss my makeup, hon." The Ham Winner tried to give Blanche a tonsil hickey. Blanche kneed him in the groin and rolled him off the stage. She pulled out a file and quickly fixed a nail. "This is quite a job for a lady. It's reduced me to a bundle of Southern fried nerves!"

Junior said, "And now on to the big prize. To show you I am the president for the people, I am gonna get a people. Whoever is selected will receive a good paying government job, working for me as my personal advisor." He leaned into his Dad and whispered. "Congressman Butts told me to listen to the people."

Junior pressed a button, and the lotto balls began to swirl around. The first number popped up. He said, "Five. The first number is five. Check your Social Security card and see if you're still in it." A few people reached for their wallets. Junior spoke up again, "The first numbers are five four six."

Chet said, "That means they're from California."

Junior said, "I hope they're from Orange County. I've got lots of supporters there. And best of all—it's the home of Disneyland. You know what? We should make Disneyland the Western White House!"

Junior announced, "We're gonna hide the last four numbers for all you identity thieves out there!"

The rest of the Social Security number popped in the chute. Chet said, "There's your number."

Junior said, "We have a winner. Now, as soon as we figure out who the lucky winner is, we'll send bring him to Washington, D.C. for a paid job to work with me. Quick, somebody go look this person up. And get me a corn dog!"

The carnival festivities continued. Back at the White House, assistants pulled up the Social Security number on the computer. Chet said, "The person you've picked is Kennedy Rutherford Jefferson."

Junior said, "Kennedy Rutherford Jefferson! Sounds like presidential material to me. Well, let's call him up and get him in here. The quicker the better. I want the people to like me."

It was a hot winter day in San Francisco, California. In the Excelsior, sometimes the neighborhood was hot whether the sun was out or not. A young woman stood at an ironing board. She wore a cooking shift over her clothes. The TV was blaring, the radio was on too, and kids were running through the house screaming. Mom was watching *Jerry Springer* and reading her Bible. Mama was yelling at the TV. "She a ho! She a big ho! Hit her again!" Kennedy was almost done ironing a blouse when the phone started to ring. She picked up her baby girl, Maleesa, and grabbed the phone in her other hand. Kennedy had a throaty, male-like voice. She said, "Hello?"

Back in the Oval Office, Junior said, "Is Kennedy Jefferson home?"

Kennedy said, "This is Kennedy Jefferson."

Junior said, "Have you been watching your television today?"

Kennedy said, "Yeah. Am I gonna win something? But damn, my Mom is watching Jerry!"

Junior spun around in the chair as he spoke on the phone. He said, "This is the president. No, not the president of Campbell's soup. Uh huh, uh huh. Okay, but there's nothing I can do if you got a bad can of mushroom soup. This is the President of the United States. It doesn't matter if you didn't vote for me—I'm still YOUR president. And I need your help."

Kennedy said, "It's about time you called." Maleesa was screaming.

Junior whispered to Chet, "He's got a kid."

Chet said, "Let's capitalize on that. Play up the old family values."

Junior held the phone away from his mouth and said to Chet, "I'll send two tickets." Then he resumed talking to Kennedy. "I'll send two tickets, please bring your child. I'd like you to fly out to the White House and be my personal assistant, be the "Voice of the People" and help me make this country great again!"

Kennedy was screaming at the kids. "Shut up! Shut up! I'm on the phone!" She looked around at the house, the kids, Mom screaming at the TV. Then she spoke again to Junior. "Is this a job?"

"Yes," Junior said.

"Does it pay?"

"Yes!" Junior said.

"Okay, I'll do it." She hung up the phone.

Kennedy said, "Hey, Mom, can you watch the kids for a while?"

Her mom didn't look up from the TV. "Yeah. Where you going?"

Kennedy said, "Washington, D.C. I got a job."

Mom said, "Shit. I thought you were going to the store. How long am I gonna be stuck with these kids?"

Kennedy adjusted the baby on her hip. She said, "I'll take Maleesa."

Mom kept talking and watching TV. "Whatchu gonna do in Washington?"

Kennedy said, "I got to get this country back on its feet."

"And how you gonna do that? You been on welfare since the day you been born. Is that how you gonna fix things?"

Kennedy's Mom always said things like that even when they weren't true. Kennedy said, "Might be. Got any money? I want to buy a new dress."

Mom wasn't happy. "You gonna go out there, and you're gonna change. They're gonna change you. They'll make you change."

"Mom. I am not gonna change."

He was hungry. He should have eaten hours ago. He wanted some chips. Potato chips. B-B-Q flavored potato chips. That's all. He could've gone to the store near his house, but he didn't. No big deal. He didn't—that was all there was to it. He'd driven halfway across town. Why? He didn't know. It had been a crazy, stressful day. He needed to do something to relax, and the chips wouldn't be enough. The SideCar? Hmmm. He'd thought about going into that bar. But no, he'd buy the chips. Maybe a can of beer—no, a bottle. A bottle of beer and some chips. That would satisfy him. A bell jingled as he walked in the store. Had anyone seen him here? Well, what if they did. He was only getting chips, that's all. Chips and a beer, just a bottle of beer. He saw himself in the video camera. Evidence. Evidence of what? Getting chips and a beer. He walked to the line of refrigerators, peered through the glass. Budweiser? Miller? Something higher end. Heineken? Maybe stick with American, Sam Adams. Who was he kidding? He didn't drink beer.

Coming here had been a mistake. He needed to get out of here. Look casual. Just buy a beer anyway. And get some chips. And get out. No one will suspect anything. Chet reached for the refrigerator door, but another man grabbed the handle first. He was a white guy in his forties with a mustache, sandy hair that fell just past his neck. His hand brushed up against his, and as it did, Chet's heart raced past the beat.

The man grabbed a six-pack of Miller then said, "Cold out today."

"Yeah," Chet said. Embarrassed, tongued-tied, he looked away, then he glanced up again.

The man ran his tongue across the edge of his mustache. "I like it hot," he said.

"Yeah," Chet said. He went to a different fridge and grabbed a six pack of soda and got his chips. He hurried to the cash register. The guy came up and stood behind him. Chet wouldn't turn and look, he wouldn't succumb, but when he looked up, they were both captured in the video camera. The guy was a bit soft in the middle, but he could see there was muscle hidden underneath. He wore jeans, tight, and Chet tried to keep his eyes from traveling to the center of the wishbone. Look at the hair! His hair looked soft. Instantly, Chet was running his hands through the sandy mop that felt like feathers. He smelled the man's hair— papaya! Oh, if only he had the guts to do it for real! His imagination was a decent second best. What must it be like to comfortably turn, ask the guy if he wanted to go to the SideCar, then actually go to the SideCar, ogle the boys, touch and be touched, then maybe land in someone's bed. Why couldn't he see THAT on the video camera? He felt like he was going to pass out. Though he tried to resist, tried to put a vise on his feelings and beat them down, he felt an emptiness in his gut. First, the pit of worry, then the rise of desire. He lowered the six pack to cover himself. He tried and tried and tried to stop it, but there was no denying it. His manhood was inspired by other men.

Tip had caught a cab and rushed over to a sound stage. He was making a commercial for Bizmark Hotels. A voiceover played as Tip, in his Rod persona, slid up around the bed with flame thrower in hand. At the end of the pitch, Rod lit the flame thrower and waved it under his chin in a psychotic, yet endearing manner.

The voiceover blared. "When Tip Murphy stays at the Bizmark, he only has to pay for Tip—his friends stay for free."

The director yelled, "Cut! Okay, take a break."

Murphy walked outside for some air. The beautiful, beautiful press were waiting.

"Mr. Vice President! Mr. Vice President!"

One media dog yelled, "Is it true Blanche has ambitions to be the First Lady?"

Murphy said, "You'll have to ask her." Murphy rolled his eyes and staggered. Suddenly Murphy was Blanche. "Now, boys, that's just rumor. So, let's squelch it right here. Rumor and innuendo, and besides, he's a married man. You know my feelings about married men. Look, but don't touch!" She pinched the air.

Murphy now took control of the body and said, "Blanche! Don't be rude. He is the president!"

Then Rod jumped in for his turn. "President! What a joke! Go on, Blanche, carry a torch for Junior... as a matter of fact, I'd like to torch his—"

Murphy interrupted, "Rod!!"

A paparazzi yelled, "Way to go, Rod!"

Chapter 12

Chet and Junior stood on the tarmac. Secret Service were scattered about, a small group of greeters and several press stood around. It was cold. What the hell were they doing outside? Just then, the airplane taxied up the runway.

Junior looked at Chet. "This is our big moment."

Chet said, "Maybe we should have sent someone to get him and escort him back to us. Then we could have a little more control over the situation."

Junior said, "No—the spontaneity. The look of surprise—it's perfect for TV."

People filed off the plane... and they kept filing, but no Kennedy. Junior was getting worried. "Where is he? Where? We should have sent someone to get him!" Chet shrugged. It was too late now. They should have made other plans, but it was too late now. Chet kept thinking that about his life. It was too late now.

Junior said, "This is terrible! What if he doesn't show up?"

The final passenger stepped out and stood at the top of the steps. It was Kennedy. She wore an African print, and her daughter wore a matching outfit.

Junior grimaced at the woman. He yelled, "Get out of my way!" Then he spoke to Chet. "These delegates from these oddball countries. They're all over the place, wearing those funny clothes and blocking my view."

The Press start snapping Kennedy's picture. They moved closer to Kennedy. Junior watched. Then the truth dawned on him.

Junior said, "Chet... you don't think that's Kennedy... do you?"

Chet said, "I think it is."

Junior said, "It's a girl, Chet. It's not a man."

Chet said, "I see."

Junior said, "It's a black girl, Chet.

Chet corrected, "A black woman."

"I thought I would get..."

Chet said, "What?"

Junior said, "Well, a white guy. A white guy in a suit. From Yale or something."

Chet said, "You wanted the 'Voice of the People.' You got it."

Junior said, "Know what, Chet? I don't think I really care what the people have to say."

Chet said, "What we have here is a major PR problem."

Kennedy walked up to Junior. Press flashbulbs sparked all over the place. Junior was so stressed, he spoke without moving his jaw.

Junior said, "Kennedy Jefferson?"

Kennedy said, "That's me."

Junior said, "I'm the president." Junior wandered off in a stupor, Kennedy followed him, a bit miffed.

Junior and Chet and Kennedy and Maleesa climbed into the limo. The car pulled away. No one spoke, and it went on like that for a while... then it went on a little longer. Finally, Junior broke the ice.

"Wow, does that rugrat need a diaper, or what?" The air in the limo was foul, and Chet looked away. Kennedy looked around, unsure of what to do. She couldn't change her in the limo.

"It was a long flight."

Junior said, "Yeah, and it's gonna be a long ride! Zowie!"

Kennedy said, "I forgot her car seat. I'll have to get one." No one spoke again until the limo pulled on the freeway. Kennedy smiled, trying to lighten the mood. "So, what am I going to do?"

Junior said, "I dunno. Do you know, Chet?" Chet just stared out the window and didn't respond. "I dunno, I thought I was getting a white guy."

Kennedy said, "What was he going to do?"

Junior responded, "Well, he was gonna, you know. Sit around and be a white guy."

That confirmed things for Kennedy. She considered several responses, then said, "Where am I going to stay?"

Junior said, "I dunno. Where's she staying, Chet?"

Chet continued to look out the window and answered, but it was a constipated mumble. "We've set up a residence for you."

"Listen, this is great!" Kennedy said. "I'm excited. A real job. It's a new start for me!" She was really trying to lighten the mood, and Chet kept thinking about his life. It was too late now.

Junior didn't know what to do, so they all drove back to the White House and went to a meeting. Junior realized he should have dropped the girl off at her residence... wherever it was... but he hadn't. And now she was sitting in the meeting, with the kid. At least the kid had a clean diaper. Junior rocked back and forth in his chair, still in a stupor. He was meeting a small committee in the Oval Office. They tried to conduct business as usual.

Carter said, "...if you really wanted to represent your constituents—"

Anderson butted in. "—I don't think you understand what I'm after here."

Kennedy listened, moving her glance from speaker to speaker. While Anderson spoke, Kennedy dropped the top of her dress and started nursing Maleesa. The committee members did their best to maintain their composure while sneaking a glance.

Carter said, "I know you're after the breast, I mean the best deal you can get for your state. But you blocked my proposal, and I'll be damned if you get your way on this one."

Anderson's eye slipped over to Kennedy's boob. He said, "Oh now let's not play tit for tat."

Junior noticed Kennedy. "What are you doing?"

Kennedy looked at him like he was nuts. "What's it look like I'm doing?"

Junior whispered to the committee members, "She's showing her breast!" Junior took a good look. He said, "She's showing her breast in the Oval Office! Caroline won't even let me take my shirt off in here!"

The staff sat, awkward, silent, embarrassed. Most of them looked down, and there was plenty of throat clearing.

131

Kennedy stared at Junior while Maleesa kept right on nursing. She said, "Got a problem?"

Junior said, "Yes, it's just like my second-grade teacher said, if there's not enough for everyone, don't take it out."

The mood in the White House Mess was boisterous. The Democrats were slapping each other on the back. Chet knew them all, but it was just a big, depressing blurry ball. One democrat said, "He's really done it this time!" Another, a female, said, "We won't have to worry about the elections this year." Another piped in, "Are you kidding? We could run Benedict Arnold and win!" They roared. What a terrific time they were having. Chet thought about how this dining room was called the White House Mess and he was in a White House mess. Chet looked at his uneaten lunch, then left.

Murphy and Wanda sat at a table, looking through the menu. "Hey, Chet!" he said, but Chet walked right on by without a hello. Tip put his attention back to the menu. "The West Wing burger looks good. I should get the fruit cup, but fries. I could go for some fries." The waiter walked over. "Afternoon, Steve. I'll have the West Wing Burger with cheddar and the fries. And an iced tea."

The waiter half bowed, "Very good, Mr. Vice President."

"I'll have the grilled chicken salad. And just water for me."

"Very good," the waiter said, half bowing and backing up to leave, then he thought better of it and spoke. "Mr. Vice President. The Geraldo Special. The one without Geraldo. It was life-changing."

"Oh, thanks, Steve, that's very kind. I appreciate   it."

The waiter looked at Wanda with envy. "You must be very proud." Wanda gave a half–smile as the waiter left.

"I need to schedule a press conference. I haven't had a press conference in two days. I need a press conference."

Wanda moved her purse to the ground then waited a moment. "I thought we could go away for a weekend. Maybe Florida. Or Rehoboth."

"They forgot to bring the bread. Maybe he's getting something special. An amuse bouche or something. "

"We could spend the time together. Just relax. Nothing fancy."

"Did I tell you I got a commercial? Nothing major, but it's something!"

"The time away will do you good. We can reconnect."

"Have you heard the GOP doesn't want to nominate Junior. Guess who they're thinking about? Me. Me. I'm gonna be the president, goddammit. All those years of toiling for the common man. They're gonna pay off. They're gonna nominate me, and how could I lose? Did you know what my approval rating is? It's eighty-six percent. Eighty-six percent. You don't see numbers like that. The whole world loves me. There's no way I could lose. If I win, at the inauguration, should I wear a suit or a dress? Maybe change halfway through? Anyway. What were you saying?"

"Nothing," Wanda said. "It was nothing. Well, there is one thing that's troubling me."

"You want to see my poll numbers in print?"

"No," she whispered. "This whole thing. This is a serious mental health issue. Not something to be made fun of."

"Made fun of?"

Wanda pointed at Tip and made a little circle in the air. "Everything about this is wrong."

"I'm not making fun of it. I'm helping them!"

"You're helping."

"Yes!" Tip held his hands out, wearing a look that read 'how can you not understand?'

"How are you helping?"

"Well... first, I've increased awareness about the issue. Now, everybody knows about multiple personalities, or as we in the field call it, Dissociative Identity Disorder. Second, I've helped increase donations to the

134

cause. Me. That's all me. I did that. And, my television appearances have made it acceptable. Even popular! So, you see, I am helping people."

"Quit fooling yourself, Tip." Then, not sure if she was talking to him or herself, Wanda said, "This isn't going to end well."

Junior ate his lunch in the Oval Office. He played with the little truck he'd gotten out of the cereal box while Fletcher marched around the room like a crazyman on a 'roid rage. Fletcher said, "There's nothing to discuss, boy! You've got to get rid of her!"

Junior said, "Dad!"

Fletcher said, "This cockamamie idea of yours is gonna sink the whole GOP."

Junior said, "It just needs a chance."

Fletcher said, "Let me put it this way—do you WANT to be re-elected?"

"You're just jealous 'cause it was my idea."

Fletcher said, "You tell me one idea of yours that ever worked?"

Junior said, "Well... that National Guard thing."

Fletcher said, "That was MY idea! Where is she now?"

"I think she went to the dining room. Everyone else is eating lunch there."

Fletcher pursed his lips, ready to speak, then he didn't speak. He rocked on his heels back and forth, trying to figure out what to say, but no words were coming. Finally, he said, "She's history. She's outta here."

Junior said, "Ah, come on, Dad."

Fletcher said, "She goes, or you go."

Junior said, "You sound just like Caroline!"

So he was fat. So what. Maybe he could do something about it, but he couldn't do anything about it right now.

His wife had packed up the kids and left. She said he drank too much and ate too much and was angry and unpleasant all the time. Every second in the house was like being chased by a bee... worrying and running, swatting the air. The house was a mess, clothes and cardboard and dirty dishes piled on the tables, the furniture, the floors. The boy was in trouble at school—bullying, and the girl, god knows what she was doing. They were behind on bills. Way behind. Three months behind on the rent, going on four. Two credit cards that had been closed, and they were getting creditor calls all the time. The place smelled of defeat.

And then there was the final night. She'd called him a loser. She'd called him every obscenity in the book, every insult she could think of, but none of them pierced him the way that word had done on the final night. She'd never called him that before.

She looked him in the eye and said it matter-of-factly: "You're a loser."

So he was fat. So what. He liked to drink, he liked to eat, he was pissed off a lot of the time. But he wasn't a loser. She hadn't said big loser, or big fat loser, just loser, and for a moment, it broke him. While he sat there broken, she packed up the kids and left. He was fat. But he wasn't a loser. Oh no, he wasn't a loser. And it was only going to take one thing to show them all. With one act, he would be a champion. Infamous. Junior Worthy was a dead man.

Chapter 13

Caroline sat in a first-grade classroom. A classroom of poor kids. Dirty, poor kids. These street urchins were cruddy. Food—milk? Maybe chocolate milk? Was smudged on their little mouths, dried and disgusting. She was sure she could hear bed bugs crawling on their low-income skin. And they smelled. Like grimy little children who had never brushed their teeth, and had been left out in the rain with a mouthful of half-digested food. She felt like she would vomit. She glanced up and saw a boy with crusted snot on the rim of his nose, she had to gulp so she wouldn't hurl. She'd paid somebody to take care of her kid. How had she gotten dragged into this miserable situation? And for this, she had dressed up? She knew this was a PR moment to encourage literacy, but there really weren't there any adults around to admire her Versace ensemble and Jimmy

Choo shoes. She always dressed like a star, and yet, he had brought this little whore into her spotlight. Why? She was younger than Caroline, slimmer, bustier, worst of all, she was something different. Her husband didn't need that type of temptation. He was an idiot, but he did have a dick, and he was always looking for a place to dunk it.

And what was the whore doing right now? Flirting with him? Dousing herself with a seductive perfume then wiggling her ample bosom right in front of his face? Maybe this whole Lotto idea was really just a way for him to get a little hoochie tail. She was going to have to do two things she really didn't want to do—one, have sex with Junior, two, set the little chippie up with someone. But who? There wasn't an eligible man for miles. But wait. There was. Of course there was. She would pair them up. And she would have to do it soon, before she found her husband spread-eagle on his desk with that slut's head in his lap.

A little white girl read from a Dr. Seuss book. The girl wore pink framed glasses, and the lenses were smudged with a million and one icky little fingerprints. The girl had a dingy pink sweater that had pilings, dingleberries, all over it. Caroline stared blankly ahead. The girl asked, "Do you like it?" Caroline didn't respond. "Do you like it?"

"No." Caroline said. "I don't like it at all." The little girl's lip quivered, then she whimpered, then she started crying. "Oh, not the book." She wished those cameras hadn't followed her here and caught that tone to her voice. "There's something else I don't like." She was going to kill that black bitch.

Junior sat at the desk in the Oval Office. It had never felt like his desk, and it still didn't. He picked up some papers. If he held papers, it looked like he was earning his money. Two Secret Servicemen stood by. Kennedy was ushered in. She sat in the chair across from him. She said, "Look, I'm here, I want to do something. I don't just want to sit at meetings being the token."

Junior said, "Nobody's toking at these meetings! They usually do that at the loading dock."

Kennedy said, "I mean I want to do something."

Junior said, "You're doing all sorts of things. Like increasing my popularity in the polls."

Kennedy said, "I am?"

Junior said, "No, actually you're sinking me like cement overshoes."

Kennedy said, "You've got me on the payroll. I want some job duties."

Junior said, "Oh. Okay. Like what?"

Kennedy said, "How should I know? Let me go visit some hospitals, or some kiddie shows. I know! Why don't I do what the First Lady does!"

Junior said, "You want to scream at me and hit me with your shoe?"

Chet poked his head in and said, "I need to speak with you."

Junior said, "Okay."

Chet said, "Alone."

Junior said, "I'll be right back." He stepped outside with Chet.

Chet said, "Did you do what your Dad said?"

"What did he say?"

"You darn well know what he said. Junior, this idea has backfired in a big way. Cut your losses. If you want any chance of getting the GOP to change their mind and nominate you, you'll have to get rid of her."

Junior said, "But, Chet!"

Chet said, "Do you want to get re-elected?"

"Why does my Dad always get his way? It's not fair." Junior re-entered the office and sat at the desk.

Kennedy said, "Sup?"

Junior said, "Some bad news. I'm afraid I'll have to let you go."

Kennedy said, "Let me go where? To Congress?"

Junior said, "There's some budget cutbacks, and we just can't afford to keep you on payroll."

Kennedy said, "What? I just got here!" She stood up and started walking around the room.

Junior said, "In the voice of the people—you're fired."

Kennedy said, "Just like that, huh?" She held on to a small marble bust.

Junior said, "Yes. You're not gonna throw that at me, are you?"

Kennedy said, "Why? Why are you dumping me? Is it because I'm a black welfare mother?"

Junior said, "You're on welfare? Oh, I am sunk."

Kennedy said, "So you're dumping me to save face. To save your big, fat, white face."

Junior said, "That kind of sums it up in a nutshell."

Kennedy said, "Don't you get it? You're being used... duped!"

Junior said, "I am?"

Kennedy said, "Yeah. You're doing it their way instead of yours."

Junior said, "Yeah. I am the president. And it was my idea. Why! They got me again! This time, I'm not gonna budge! My idea's gonna work."

Kennedy said, "It will work. But I need to be doing something! A job. A role."

Junior said, "I brought you here to advise me."

Kennedy said, "Advise you on what?"

Junior said, "I don't know. The country!"

Kennedy said, "Okay... what do you want to know?"

Junior said, "How can we make it better?"

Kennedy said, "I don't know."

Junior said, "I thought two heads were better than one. How are we going to get anywhere if you're as dumb as me?"

Kennedy said, "I ain't dumb!" She was pissed. "I am not dumb!"

Junior knew the look. "Oooh. Sore point. Owie! I touched something that hurts." Then he said in a sing-song fashion, "Somebody's touchy about being called dumb!"

Kennedy said, "If I'm dumb, then you're a goddamn idiot!!"

"Look, I'm the president, and if you're gonna call me names, you can just get out!" Junior said.

Kennedy said, "Wait, that's it! I got it! If you and me can get along, we can, like, show the whole country that different kinds of people can get along."

Junior said, "And what will that do?"

Kennedy said, "It can start solving a big problem. Racism and how people hate each other."

Junior said, "I really don't follow you."

Kennedy said, "Don't you think that's important?"

143

Junior said, "It was never a problem in my neighborhood."

Kennedy said, "Well it's a big problem in this country, and you and me can start to fix it."

Junior said, "I don't have to touch anybody, do I?"

Kennedy moved closer, then touched him. She said, "Maybe me. We got this country with all these different kinds of people—you know, Chinese and Latino and Native American. Let's show they're worth something, starting with you respecting me. Someone white respecting someone black."

Junior said, "Well, I already have Chet."

Kennedy said, "I said someone black. You wanted advice? Let's pull the people of this country together. That'll get you re-elected."

Junior said, "It will? Dammit, you're a genius! I don't care what anyone says. You're staying on!"

Just then, Murphy stuck his head through the door. "Did you want to see me?"

"No," Junior said.

"Are you sure?" Murphy asked, and he walked into the Oval Office and sat down. "Have you seen my poll numbers? Eighty-six percent approval rating. Can you believe it? Eighty-six percent approval. I've never seen anything like it. I can do no wrong. How are your numbers?"

144

"I don't know," Junior said. He sat at his desk and started pouting. He knew his numbers and they were in the gutter.

"I've heard they're not so great. Not so great. I've heard bad news. That the convention may not make you the nominee. Have you heard that?"

"No," Junior said.

"Have you heard who the leading contender is? It's me! Eighty-six percent. Eighty-six percent! How can I fail?"

"It's okay," Kennedy said. "We're gonna turn it around. We're gonna show the country that Junior can be the best president ever. We're gonna get that nomination."

"Hmm. And how are you going to do that."

"Junior and me—we're gonna show people that whites and blacks can get along, we're gonna face it head on, and we're gonna end racism."

"That's interesting."

"Yeah," Junior said. "That's not something you could do. You don't have a black employee... or, friend, or... Murphy, do you even know anyone who is black?"

"Yeah, you couldn't make a difference in race relations," said Kennedy.

Murphy brushed a few breadcrumbs off his lapel. "Well... I don't know all my different personalities, but I think—I'm not sure—I think one of them might be black. My

145

own personality might be able to help me build a bridge between the races, especially if both races are me, but I can't really control things, if—!"

Murphy stopped, and it looked like was choking, then he fell into a trance.

"What the hell?" said Kennedy.

"Oh, he's transforming!" said Junior. "Who are you?"

"I'm Tyrone," said Murphy.

Kennedy sneered and rolled her eyes. "Oh great, here we go. We're gonna get a tired, ghetto stereotype of 'Tyrone' the old-G."

"But my friends call me Reverend." Murphy sprang up, raising his hands, ready to preach, then he let loose in a sing-song style. "You know, I love the Lord! And I love to sing! The Lord, don'tchu know he can solve every problem. He has solved, yes, he has, he has solved every one of mine: A-ay-men! Let me, let me tell you about one of those problems. You know, I was tired, yes, I was, I was tired of my lady. Oh yes, Lord, Lordy, Lord! We'd been together too long, way, way too long. And it was just like a worn-out recording, so worn-out, a worn-out recording of a favorite song... Gimme a Hallelujah! Hallelu! Hallelujah!"

Kennedy struggled with what he was saying. "That sounds familiar."

"It must be from the Bible. He's a Reverend and all."

"That's not the Bible!" Kennedy said.

Murphy kept singing in his black preacher persona. "So, while she lay there sleeping, I went on and I read the paper, yes I did, I read the paper in bed. And in the personal columns, personal! There was this letter I read. Yes, I did. I read it. And it said, and it said, the letter said, oh yes, Lord, the letter said—if you like Pina Coladas! Gimme an Amen!"

"Of course. The Pina Colada song," said Kennedy

"And getting caught in the rain, if you're not into, not into yoga, and if you have half a brain, if you like making love at midnight, say Hallelujah!"

"Hallelujah!" said Junior.

"Don't egg him on," said Kennedy.

"What's that, Lord? What's that? You want me to run, to make a run for the presidency? Oh mercy, Lord, I'm not the man. I don't have your wisdom to guide the people. What's that, Lord? I'm the chosen one? I can help pull our country together? Heal our racial wounds? And develop a strong economy? Hallelujah, Lord! Tell me, Lord, if you like Pina Coladas! Oh, Lord, if it's your will. If it's your will for me to lead this country. Thy will be done! Amen! Gimme an Amen!"

"Amen!" said Junior, and Kennedy gave him a punch.

Murphy tried doing a dance, but slipped, then fell to the floor.

"What happened?" said Junior, and Murphy started to crawl up, a bit hazy.

"Where am I?" Murphy said.

"You're in the Oval Office," said Junior.

"I feel like I blacked out."

"You were Tyrone."

"Tyrone."

"The singing black preacher. Man, you're the chosen one!"

"I'm not the chosen one... I'm just Tip Murphy. But eighty-six percent. If I... if Tyrone and I can serve this country by healing our racial divide, then I'm willing to do it!"

Kennedy looked at Murphy. "He's just a big old faker."

"A big old faker—who's the chosen one," said Junior.

"Who has an eighty-six percent approval rating," said Murphy, then he added, as Tyrone, "A-a-a-a-men!"

Chapter 14

Donaldson's face looked like it was ready to explode. "What was that? What was that?"

Fat Ass dropped his head. "It was a good idea. Poorly executed."

"It was an awful idea. And those pants had to be three sizes too small! He was in the palm of your hand. And you blew it."

"I have another idea."

"Enough of your ideas." He wondered about Fat Ass. Had he really ever done a successful hit? Why couldn't he have gotten Long Dong? Fat Ass had probably been a fat boy in high school who had shied away from being social, who had sweated his way through college until he dropped out then finally found a niche—a niche that he couldn't keep. Donaldson had no confidence in Fat Ass's skills. Maybe he should dump him now. And even if he could trust his skills, could he trust Fat Ass to keep his mouth shut? Would the Fat One be successful, then spill his guts to a tabloid for cash, or just for the celebrity? Maybe this was a bad idea.

"I've been having second thoughts. I want to call it off."

"What?"

"Break the contract."

"No. No! I can do this. You just have to give me a chance!"

"You've had several chances, and he's still here. You're incompetent! And I don't think that's going to change."

"It's changed. Believe me. I've changed. I have a reason now. It's as important to me as it is to you to see him dead!"

"Keep your voice down!" Donaldson whispered through gritted teeth. How badly was he putting his soul on the line? "One chance. That's it. If you can't pull it off next time, that's it. Over."

"You won't regret it," Fat Ass said. "You will not regret this."

Fletcher Worthy walked into the Oval Office. He wore his cowboy hat, a tan Stetson, his cowboy boots, a pair of black beauties with a three-row stitched design in red and white and inlaid uppers, with a buckaroo style heel. He had on a belt with a fat, silver belt buckle worthy of Elvis and a turquoise ring made in a bear paw style. He said a Navajo Chief had bestowed the ring on him in thanks of his public service, but really he had bought it at the Phoenix airport. Fletcher bit and sucked on a cigar.

"Well, son. Did you fire her?"

Junior looked out the window and didn't answer for several seconds. Finally, he spoke. "No."

"Oh, so you need a little help. Your ole' Dad has no problem firing people."

"I don't need your help."

"All right. All right. I'll let you do this on your times-table. Let the girl have a final meal before you pack her up and send her back."

"I'm... I'm not gonna do it," Junior said.

"You're not gonna do what?"

"I'm not gonna do it. I'm not gonna fire her."

"What?" Fletcher was mystified. "I told you to."

"No."

"What did you say?"

"I said no, Dad."

"But I told you to do it."

"And I said no."

"You've never said no before."

"I'm saying it now. NO."

Fletcher stood for a minute. He looked out the window. He looked at the Oval Office

151

rug with its eagle and arrows. Then he looked Junior in the eye. "You're gonna regret you ever said that, son. You don't tell me no. You're going to be sorely disappointed" Fletcher looped his thumbs behind the belt buckle and slowly sauntered out. He looked over his shoulder as he walked out. "Sorely disappointed."

Junior and Caroline were in bed. Caroline read a book while Junior rubbed his index finger against the lace of her nightgown. "I was thinking, honey. Remember that movie we saw? The one in the gym? The one where the lat machine pole was going in and out and in and out of the hole? And then the muscleman went all spread eagle on the weight bench? And then the girl, you know, she went downtown? I was thinking maybe you might want to try—"

"I told you, I'm not going to do that! I'm a good girl." But maybe she wouldn't be able to be a good girl for long. Maybe, if she wanted to keep her husband, she was going to have to break down and—no! Just the thought of it made her want to throw up. Good girls don't do that.

"Honey, there's nothing wrong with going oral." She wanted to hit him. "Bill Clinton did it, and he was president. Bill Clinton probably did it in this very bed.

Probably not with Hillary, but I bet he did it right here."

"I'm not going to put my mouth there."

"Well, you don't have to."

"Good."

"Why don't you just let me do you?"

"I said No! Plus, it's that time of the month."

"You mean the time you don't let me touch you?"

"Look, I was thinking…"

Junior said, "I was thinking too, but that's as far as it ever gets."

"We should have a dinner party. A state dinner."

"Okay."

"Couples only."

"All right." Junior seemed to drop off to sleep. "Oh, honey, but what about Chet?"

"Maybe you could find him a date."

"Okay. But the only girl I know is you."

"Maybe you'll think of someone."

"Okay."

"Maybe someone who is new. In your office. A girl."

"Maybe I could hire someone…"

"What about Kennedy?"

"Oh! I know! Kennedy! The new girl! She's a girl! AND she's black! I think Chet will like that! This is terrific! A dinner party, and we'll have dancing!"

Caroline put her book on the nightstand. Kennedy would be out of the picture soon enough. Let her throw herself at Chet and cling all over him. Chet was perfect. He had no one and, though he had so much more class than Kennedy did, Kennedy was a girl, and Chet had a penis. The hard part was over. Now she could plan on what to wear.

"Hon, this state dinner is a great idea! Let's get a karaoke machine!"

Junior and Chet jogged around the White House, followed by Secret Service agents. Junior said, "I've made a big decision."

Chet said, "Finally! I'm so glad to hear you're putting the country's needs first. Is it about replacing Lincoln's head? About the economy? About that new Middle East situation? What's the decision?"

"I'm having a dinner party."

Chet said, "The whole country wants to throw you out of office and all you can think of doing is having a dinner party? Is this smart?"

Junior said, "Chet, this is what presidents do! And, if I don't get re-elected at least I will have had a good time." Junior was winded and stopped for a breather. "Chet, you've got to do me a favor."

Chet said, "What now?"

Junior said, "You know, we're having this big dinner and all, and well... I was wondering if you could take Miss Jefferson to the dinner. She needs an escort, and I was thinking, well, you always go by yourself to those things, and maybe you'd like to take a girl for once."

Chet said, "What? She's half my age! And... I wouldn't want her to get the wrong idea."

Junior said, "It's only a date, okay? I'm not asking you to marry her."

Chet said, "Let me think about it."

Junior said, "I'll spring for gas."

Chet said, "All right. Could you ask her to wear something a little more modest?"

Junior said, "You got it, Chetsky. I'll ask her to wear something to cover up those curves. And by curves, I mean boobs. Boy, Deja vu! This is just like when I had to set my cousin up."

Murphy and Wanda sat at a table in the Ballot Box. Murphy was sizing up that what was left of his drink was mostly ice, with maybe one last gulp left. Then, from the corner of his eye, he saw his commercial coming on the TV set that hung near the end of the bar.

Murphy stood up and yelled, "Hey, guys, quiet down! Here's my commercial!" The crowd turned to the TV to watch the commercial. On the tube, Tip walked in the door of a room at the Bizmark Hotel carrying his luggage. He smiled directly at the camera

155

as his other personas appeared. Rod slithered up the bed, then ignited his flame thrower, Blanche sipped a cup of tea on the edge of the bed, Mikey jumped up and down on the bed. The commercial voice over kicked in, "When Tip Murphy stays at the Bizmark, he only has to pay for Tip—his friends stay for free."

The crowd at the Ballot Box broke into applause, yelling and laughing, people yelled, "Hey, why couldn't you get a beer commercial?"

"Good work."

"Way to go, Tip."

"Thank you, thank you!" Murphy said. He sat back down, then smiled at Wanda. "Pretty good, huh? It's amazing how they can do all those special effects."

Wanda glared at him. "Not to mention your own special effects."

Murphy said, "I believe we already finished this conversation."

Wanda really wanted a cigarette. "You've got it made. Whenever you screw up, you can blame it on Rod. It's the perfect situation for a politician."

The glaring was turning into a stare-down when Donaldson walked over. He looked from Murphy to Wanda, then spoke. "Good to see you Murphy... Wanda."

Wanda welcomed the interruption. "Hi, Jim. Would you like to join us?"

Murphy said, "No, he wouldn't."

Donaldson pulled out the chair with an annoying screech. "Don't mind if I do. Nice commercial, Tip."

Murphy said, "Thanks. Hey, and that's nothing. I got one coming up for Nike and one for McDonalds."

Donaldson took the plastic toothpick from Murphy's drink and ate the cherry stabbed on the end. "That's great... too bad it's a big sham."

Murphy swatted the toothpick out of Donaldson's hand, then spoke as Blanche. "Why, Jim, darlin', I just don't know what you mean."

Donaldson looked at him, picked up Murphy's drink and polished it off. "Sure you do, Blanche. Have a good evening." Donaldson got up and left.

Wanda picked up Murphy's empty glass, looked at it, then put it back on the table. She stared at the glass for half a second until she couldn't contain it any longer and blurted it out. "I told you so."

Murphy looked away. Then, softly, he said, "Shut up," then he gulped down Wanda's drink.

Chapter 15

Junior, Chet, and Fletcher sat in the Oval Office. Fletcher sat at the desk with his boots on the desk, with Junior and Chet flanking him. Fletcher sucked his teeth with a toothpick, then, finally, he spoke. "Well, if you're keeping her, what do we do with her?"

Junior said, "Why don't we let her talk to kids?"

Chet shook his head. "No kids."

Junior continued. "Maybe she could be, like, the White House Oprah."

"Son. You're an idiot."

Chet said, "You know... that might work. You wanted the voice of the people. Maybe people could come and voice their thoughts to her."

Junior added, "Then we could turn it into a talk show!"

Chet said, "Let's stick with just an office for now. Maybe we can turn this debacle around."

Fletcher said, "Listen to that mouth! Debacle! And you got mad when I called her the n-word!"

Chet paused, then spoke. "You know, guys, you make it really hard to work here... But let's solve this. We'll need to train her. How to not to lose her cool. How to respond. How to be empathetic without making promises. This just might work."

It was a room. Not huge, but more than she'd ever had. There was a desk. Solid wood. They had let her pick out office supplies from a catalog. She was even going to get to decorate and had picked out several inspirational posters and they were even going to come framed. Plus, someone had already hung a picture of Martin Luther King. She knew she could make a difference—she'd just never had the chance. This was the chance... she was going to turn it into something big.

An intern escorted a woman into the room. "This is Miss Parker. She'll be helping... uh, train you." Miss Parker was a white lady with curly hair, not blonde but not red.

"Nice to meet you. What is that hair color?"

"Oh, it's strawberry blonde!" She smiled, showing her perfectly straight teeth. Her little button of a nose crinkled. Strawberry blonde. Now that was something only white folks would ever know about. And maybe this job... maybe this job was something only white folks could ever know about. Kennedy had dropped out of high school... she'd been smart too. Everyone said she was the smart one in the family. And she was almost done. It'd been was March, there had only been about two months left, and one day, she'd woken up, and the twins were crying, and her mom was yelling and praying at the TV, and it was a day like every day, but something inside her had clicked off. She didn't get out of bed. The alarm went off, the gangsta rap pleading with her to get of bed. But she didn't. And it didn't matter, really. It was only one day. She'd go tomorrow. But she didn't. She didn't go the next day or the next or the next. Her friends had called, but mostly to talk about boys. The school called for a while, mostly her counselor, but Kennedy wouldn't pick up the phone. The counselor had talked to her mother.

Kennedy had a plan. She was going to go to Merritt College. Study business. She and Damian could get married. She'd go to work. Maybe start her own business one day. Then, one day, that idea had washed away, like her name carved in the sand, smudged out by the bay waters. She'd been trying to raise her kids and make it on the little she got from the state and her part-time job at Popeye's. Who was she kidding? She couldn't do this work. She couldn't fit in at The White House. The White House! But she could take their money. Sit there and pretend she knew what she was doing. She was the smart one! Maybe she could do it. Maybe there was still time to learn. Stop! She had to stop this thinking. She could do it. She had to make the most of this chance.

"How does that sound?" Miss Parker asked with her blinding smile. She sure smiled a lot. Already, Kennedy had missed what she'd said. Should she ask Parker to tell her again or just agree with her?

"That sounds good."

"Let's start with the basics. Remember, it's greet, listen, respond. It's very simple!" Kennedy thought Parker's dimples were about to crush her entire face. This Parker was a real people pleaser. Kennedy had never been that type. She wondered what Parker was like in bed—huge smile, telling her man how satisfying he was when he really had a pencil dick. *"Oh, you're good, that's good, that feels so good! I love you, honey!"* Smiling the entire time, whether she could feel his dick pounding in her or not.

"First, I'll play your part! So, you'll come in and tell me about one of your concerns."

Or maybe in bed, Parker's real self came to life. Maybe she wore one of those black, lace-up pleather suits and forced her man to go down on her while she whipped him with a riding crop. Maybe that was the only time she smiled for real. Or maybe the smile fell off then, turning into a drooling, open-mouth gape. Gape! She knew the word gape. She could do this job.

"Hi, I'm Kennedy."

"Make up a name!" Miss Parker put her on edge. She wasn't going to give up. She was willing to go through whatever it took to get good at this.

"Hi, I'm Janneese."

"Hi, Janice, I'm Kennedy. I'm our nation's goodwill ambassador to the voice of our country's people!!"

"Do I have to say that?"

"Play along!"

"Nice to meetcha."

"So, what's your concern."

"Well...um. The store by my house."

"Yes?"

"It carries expired milk." Kennedy grimaced.

"Uh huh?"

"And they try to hide it by turning the date to the back."

"I see."

"It's not right. The people in my neighborhood. Our babies. They don't need to drink spoiled milk."

"Is that it?"

"Yeah."

"All righty! Well, Miss Janice, I hear what you're saying—this is very important—and it pains me to know that our nation's little babies might be getting sour milk. I'm going to look into this. It's been terrific meeting you!"

When Parker said 'hear' she touched her ear, when she said 'important,' she cupped her chin, when she said 'pains,' she touched her heart. At 'terrific meeting you,' she had grabbed Kennedy by the hand and was leading her to the door. This was bullshit. Kennedy dropped her hand. "Yeah, but what you gonna do about it?"

Parker was caught off guard. "What?"

"What you gonna do about it?"

Parker broke character. She waggled her index finger at Kennedy and whispered, "We don't make promises."

"This is bullshit. I'm not gonna play with people. Listen to their problems then kick they asses out the door."

"Now you try!" Parker pretended to walk in the door. "Hi, I'm Beverly Patton."

"Hi."

"Say nice to meet you, Beverly."

"Nice to, nice to meet you, Beverly."

"So, what's your concern?"

"I thought I was supposed to say that."

"You are. I was just reminding you."

Kennedy waited a second. Should she go on, or just kick this girl's ass? "So, what's your concern?"

"Hmm…. Let's see." Parker thought for many seconds, then excitedly had an answer. "Oh, the last time I flew to Paris, I had just bought a latte, and they made me throw it away. Maybe we can do something about the regulations that don't allow a latte past airport security."

Kennedy took a minute to think this through. Her problem was she was going to Paris—Paris, France? And she didn't get to bring her fancy coffee through security. Kennedy was used to different problems. Security pulling guns on friends. People getting shot or stabbed on BART. Damian getting killed. Cops pulling over her friends for driving while brown… Not a lot of issues with traveling to France. How to respond?

"That's your problem? Bitch, please! A rich ho like you's got nothin' to complain about. Buy your goddamn latte after you get through security, dumbass."

"Okay, that's not bad. Now let's try this. I hear what you're saying…" She touched her ear.

Caroline felt a little flutter in her diaphragm. What was that feeling? She was giddy, that was it. She hadn't felt giddy for a decade! She was pleased she'd come up with an idea to pry Kennedy from her husband, but she hadn't expected the thrill of planning the state dinner. There was so much to do—choosing the menu, the place settings, the décor, the entertainment. Of course, since it was a state dinner, she needed an international leader. She had hoped for a royal, but with the late notice, it just wasn't possible. But she'd found someone—The president of Slovakia. He was interested, available, and alive. She was supposed to select a five-course meal that reflected the culture of Slovakia. Well, what on earth would that be? Probably filet. Anyone from these poor countries would like a filet. A filet and scalloped potatoes. Two courses down. And cheesecake for dessert. Everyone loves that. Damn, she should have been a professional party planner! Who should entertain? She'd already been turned down by three A-list singers, but she'd find someone. And the china—should she use the gold or the blue and white porcelain? So many choices! It was exhilarating. She should have a state dinner every day.

"How's the liver?"

"It's not jaundiced yet, but I keep working at it." Murph held up his glass in a toast. "Here's to Sir!" He took a pause. "Cirrhosis!" He took a gulp. "Oh, you mean my lunch. This is the best liver and onions I've ever had. Want a bite?"

"No thanks." Wanda paused, then started again. "Do you even go into work anymore? Your office? The Senate?"

"When they need me, I do. Otherwise, it's pressers, it's filming commercials, that sort of thing."

"Murph... I'm not very demanding. I'm not high-maintenance."

"You're right." He shoveled another bite of the liver into his mouth.

"Can I ask you one favor?"

"Of course, Wanda, you know I'd do anything for you."

"During the state dinner... can you please not go into character."

"Go into character? They're not characters. I have no control over it."

"You know what I mean. I just want one night. Of normal."

Murph rested his fork on the table. "Sure. One night."

"One night. Thank you."

"Wanda. I really love you. You're everything to me."

And with that, Wanda knew they could get back to where they'd been. He would drop the silly routine, and they would retire to Florida. And it might not be happily ever after, but it would be ever after. She had done it. She had pulled him back to reality.

Chet ran his finger across the spreadsheet. "If you look at these figures, you'll see the change in the economic growth rate."

"What figures? Those look like numbers."

"Okay..."

"Chetarella, are you ready for the state dinner? Did you rent a tux?"

"I own a tux."

"You OWN a tux? Wow. You are the man." Junior ran his finger across the numbers on the spreadsheet. "I ran my finger, but I don't get it."

"Don't worry. I'm going to come up with another idea."

"Thanks again for taking Kennedy to the party. I really appreciate it."

"I'm always here to do my duty."

"You're lucky. She sure is... different."

"Different than what?"

"Different than Caroline. Something different."

"Whatever that means."

"She has... she has big boobs, Chet." Junior thought for a second. "I like big boobs."

"I hadn't really noticed."

"Oh, well, they're big. You should notice. They're plenty big. I think they're like Triple-Ds."

"She's still nursing. I think it does that."

"I'd like to nurse those big bazongas... Caroline is a 32-B. And she never lets me touch them. They're always barricaded in a Playtex 18-hour bra. And she won't wear anything sexy, it looks like a gauze wrapping! I bet Kennedy will wear a lacy bra with underwire to hold those big melons up. Or maybe a peekaboo bra... Or satin! Do you think you'll get to second base, Chet? You'll have to tell me what it's like when you squish those bodacious tatas."

"I'm going to try and be a gentleman."

"Okay. Can you be a gentleman and get a picture?"

Chapter 16

The driver pulled the SUV up to Kennedy's apartment. Chet walked out, flanked by Secret Service. He rang the bell, and Kennedy opened the door. She wore a form-fitting, floor length, black gown.

Chet took her in. "You look beautiful."

"Thanks," Kennedy said.

"I got you this." He handed her an orchid.

Kennedy said, "Nice tux. You look like Muggsy."

Chet said, "Who's Muggsy?"

Kennedy said, "The guy who took me to my junior prom."

Chet said, "I'll take that as a compliment."

Kennedy said, "That was a great time! There was a lot of stress too... finding the right dress... coming up with the money for everything... getting a sitter for my kids. They had it on this boat on the bay. It was great. I got so drunk, I threw up off the side of the boat. Muggsy fell overboard. But they got him. What was your prom like?"

Chet said, "I didn't go."

Kennedy said, "That's too bad."

Chet said, "Couldn't go, actually."

Kennedy said, "Oh. Did you live in the south or something and try and take a white girl?"

Chet said, "No."

Kennedy said, "It was the money, huh? That's the way it is with everyone."

Chet said, "We should get going."

The SUV ride was uncomfortable. Chet looked out the window. Kennedy looked out the window. The silence was deafening. Finally, Kennedy spoke. "Have you worked a long time?"

Chet nodded. "Since I got out of college."

"But how many years?"

"That would be more than twenty." Kennedy looked nervous. Chet felt sorry for her. He would like to help her out, but how?

"This is really my first real job and... well, when you first started working, did you find yourself thinking about sex all the time?"

"Um... it's hard to remember that long ago."

"What about now? Do you ever think about sex instead of your job?"

"Quite honestly, I spend most of my time thinking about how I'm going to keep my job."

Kennedy looked out the window again. "You must think I am so ghetto!"

The honor guards and color guards in full dress uniform stood at attention. Junior and Caroline Worthy stood at the North Portico entrance of the White House, waiting to greet the president of Slovakia. For all of Caroline's desire to live in color, she had selected another beige gown. She just couldn't let go of her past. The motorcade drove up, and President Michel Varga and his wife, Kveta, walked out. There was a brief photo op at the top of the staircase, then Junior and Caroline escorted President and Mrs. Varga to the Yellow Oval Room for the evening reception.

Chet stood next to Junior, feeding him the names of the guests, as well as the bacon wrapped date appetizers. Junior had already downed three glasses of champagne. Caroline kept a big, fake smile plastered on her face and drifted next to her husband. "Lay off the sauce, Peanut," she said to him. "And eat something besides bacon. Booze and bacon. Your blood sugar's going to be a disaster."

After the pictures and the anthems

and the receiving line, they finally made it to the State Dining Room. Before the five-course meal could begin, both presidents were to deliver a speech. Varga went first, and for about twenty minutes, talked about how all countries, but especially Slovakia and the United States, could work toward world peace while tackling other challenges including poverty and economic inequity. Then it was Junior's turn. He was a bit restless at the podium. An aide handed him the prepared speech.

"Well, I am really, really hungry, and we don't get to eat until the speech is done, so I'm gonna go off the speech and just speak from my heart." He cleared his throat. "Trick or treat, smell my feet, give me something good to eat. Thank you."

Junior sat down. Varga had stared at the podium and continued to stare at it, then he picked up the dessert spoon and looked at his reflection.

"So, how long have you been king of...."

"Slovakia. I'm not the king. I'm the president."

"So, the king appointed you president."

"I was elected. We're a democracy."

"So, your people are starving. And we're going to give you money."

"Slovakia has one of the strongest economies in Europe. We have universal health care, free education, a comprehensive Social Security system, and one of the longest paid maternity leaves in the world."

"Yeah, but you're called Slovakia. It just sounds... poor."

"Do you know anything about my country?"

"Ummm... the Marx Brothers made a movie about it?"

"That was Freedonia!"

"Okay, then I guess the answer is no. I don't know anything about your country."

"Maybe that's a good thing."

Caroline had ditched the idea of the filet and had selected lobster. When it arrived, Kennedy said, "Wow! I love lobster!" Kennedy picked up the lobster and pulled the claw off with her hands and took a bite. She said, "Damn! This is good!" She turned and yelled, "Hey, is this place all you can eat?" She whispered to Chet, "I'm gonna put one of these in my purse."

Chet was mortified. "Miss Jefferson. Miss Jefferson. There's a formal way to eat a lobster."

A few members of the press came over. "You look beautiful, Miss J! Kennedy grabbed Chet and posed with the lobster. The press bulbs popped while Kennedy tried different poses as Chet tried to pull away.

Across the table, Murphy slid his hand up Wanda's leg. She gazed at him. He winked at her then tossed back his scotch. She was satisfied. She felt calm. He was back. Florida. It was all going to work out. The Press moved over to Murphy and it was as if a spell was cast. It was as if Wanda slid off the planet, and he was pulled into the light, the flash of the cameras. It was hypnosis, psychosis, cirrhosis.

One of the press members shouted, "Oh look, it's Mikey!"

Another photog said, "Hi, Mikey! Say something cute!"

And in that instant, it was all gone. He relapsed. That alluring flash mesmerized him into Mikey, the five-year-old boy. Murphy, as Mikey, said, "Uh oh! I tink I pee peed my pants!" The press, and everyone around, loved it. They laughed and clapped. It was so cute! Everyone loved it, everyone except one person. Murphy grinned and twisted his fingers. The flashes went wild, and the more they popped, the cuter he got. Wanda watched Murphy, then she took a gulp from her drink and looked down.

Caroline had a hard time finding entertainers. Again, the short notice, everyone was scheduled, and it was challenging to get someone to come to Washington, D.C. in the winter. But she'd finally landed a very popular act—a group called Fly With Me. They had several hits, well, two hits, in the 80s, and they were still

174

very popular. It was two men and two women, and the men dressed as airline captains and the women dressed as stewardesses. It was very fun. That's what she kept telling Junior. All their songs had some sort of airline reference, and it was just charming. In an 80s sort of way.

The instrumental was digital, and it blared through the speakers. The four ran out, doing a sort of slow running man that turned into jumping jacks when they hit the stage. They wore sky-blue uniforms, the captains with military caps and stripes on their arms while the women had short skirts and cute little hats that barely perched on their big coifs. The men carried lighted landing batons, and the colors in the batons changed and seemed to dance along with the music. The women had small trays with a plastic bottle of champagne and plastic champagne glasses glued to the tray so they could swing without a spill. The choreography was ancient and corny, and when the cue hit, they sang.

> Skooch over here!
> And give me a nice, back rub
> The blue skies are clear!
> When we join the mile-high club!

Junior looked at them then said, "Wow. Even I know this is horrible." Junior jumped on the stage. "C'mon, everybody—

time to dance." He shoved the Fly With Mees out of the way and shouted to Caroline. "What's that song I like?"

"Oh no. Not Achy Breaky Heart."

"That's it!" Junior grabbed the mic and sang words, but not the words to the song. "Ache! Break! I know this, cuz it's Achy. Yes, it's the Achy broken heart, oh it makes me cry, don't break my ache, get me some painkillers, cause I'm achy! C'mon honey!"

Caroline said, "Junior, sit down!"

Junior said, "Sit down? I'm on a roll!" He started dancing on the stage. "Come on, people, let's get a conga line going!" No one moved. "Look, I'm the president, and I say— Conga Line!" Reluctantly, people dragged themselves from their chairs and built a sorry, unhappy conga line. Junior led the line and shouted on the cordless mic. "Conga, conga, conga! Conga, conga, conga!" The president of Slovakia looked sorrowful. He didn't have much rhythm, but he did his best to kick right, then left.

Caroline did not get up. She had planned this dinner to get Kennedy out of the picture... but once she got started with the planning, well... it was just everything she was living for—the preparation, the choices, the thrill, and now it was all going down the toilet with a stupid husband-induced conga line! Caroline felt a tiny part of her heart break. Omigod! She had the achy breaky heart! She wiped a tear from her eye. She had brought a large handbag and now opened it to reveal why. Inside, her crown. Quietly, she slipped it on. She held her arm out and up, a bit like the royal wave, and she sat, regally, queen of all the conga lines she saw.

Kennedy and Chet slowly moved up the walk that led to Kennedy's apartment. "Well, this is it." She waited, wondering if he was going to kiss her and if his mouth action was as square as the rest of him. She turned the key. "Why don't you come inside?"

"I don't want to wake the baby. And the Secret Service. They're tired."

"It's all right. She sleeps through the night. Come on in, just for a drink. Tell the Secret Service to stuff it."

Chet hesitated. "I really shouldn't. I need to go. Big day tomorrow."

Kennedy put her hands on her hips and gave him some attitude. "What's wrong with you anyway?

Chet said, "Well, I'll stay for one drink."

Kennedy took care of the sitter and brought in a bottle of wine and two glasses. Chet looked at the label. "Oh. I didn't know they had vineyards in San Francisco."

"Yeah, and what's terrific about this one is they put a booster in it to jack up the alcohol content."

Chet hesitated. "Did you just say terrific?"

Kennedy pulled off her dress, revealing a tight-fitting shell underneath. She looked good and she knew it. Chet was sweating uncomfortably on the couch. She figured he'd want to be the good little politician boy, but with the right moves, he'd crack and go for it. She squeezed a little closer.

Kennedy said, "You're cute."

Chet said, "I really should be going."

Kennedy said, "A man like you... successful... good looking... a guy like you oughta be married.

Chet stared at his glass. "Well, it's got a bit of a bite..." He took another sip. "Maybe it's more like a pit bull—grabs you by the neck and won't let go."

Kennedy said, "What was it? You had a girl once and she used you?"

That was enough. Chet set the glass down and stood up. "Look, I'm almost twice your age and... I really should be getting home."

Kennedy said, "What is it? You're scared of women? You're a virgin?"

Chet was clearly offended. "I'm uh... I'm uh... well, private about my personal life."

"Private?"

"Yes, I... I...."

178

Then it clicked in her head. Kennedy said, "Oh... you like men."

Chet had never acknowledged it, so why should he now? But he had sold Kennedy short. She was so different from him... but he liked her. He trusted her. "There's nothing wrong with it."

She sighed. "There is if I was planning on sleeping with you. Oh well. I shoulda known. I guess everybody knows."

Chet said, "Everybody who needs to know knows."

Kennedy said, "Junior?"

Chet said, "He doesn't know. And he'll never figure it out. Really, no one knows. I hope this can remain confidential between us."

Kennedy said, "You must have the wrong idea about me. I'm not gossip. I'm no blabbermouth!"

"Thank you."

"How many men have you been with?"

Chet just sat there, biting his lip.

"Oh... you've never been with anyone."

Chet got up and headed for the door. "Well, thank you. It's been a lovely evening."

The door shut. It hadn't been a lovely evening. It had been a horny, unsatisfying evening! Damn, he had to be gay. She should have guessed!

Chapter 17

Luckily, they had a mirror she could check right before she entered the room. She looked herself in the eye and thought *Don't mess this up.* She would have thought a different word, but they had told her to keep the language rated-G. This was it, this was her big chance. The strawberry haired chick—what was that girl's name? No matter. Strawberry Hair kept calling the audience diverse. That was white code for black and brown people. Kennedy was gonna do this! She was gonna shine! The nerves. Her stomach was flip-flopping. She took a step back and looked at herself in the mirror. She didn't even recognize the person looking back. The had put an old black lady wig on her, covering her braids. The wig was straightened and ended in a curl at the bottom. Who did she look like with that hair? It seemed familiar, but she couldn't quite place it. Oh God! It was Mother Goose! She was the black Mother Goose!

And they had put her in these beige granny hose, with chunky low-heeled shoes. They had picked out everything. A boxy navy-blue suit that wasn't her at all. She thought of her neighbor, Mrs. Jensen, heading off to teach Sunday School. She wore suits like this, with the military shoulders and a hemline past the knee. Oh well, it wasn't her, but it was what she had to do to make this work. It was temporary. "They'll change you." That's what her mother had said, but this was only the outside. She was still Kennedy.

She had to show them she could do it. They were all snobby rich kids who had grown into snobby rich adults, but she had to show them she was as good as they were. She could hold her own. None of these White House staffers would understand the life she'd had. No money, no opportunity, and not much hope. After Damian was killed, things had gotten really bad. She couldn't talk to anyone here about that. They wouldn't understand. He was in the wrong place at the wrong time. If that hadn't happened, things might be different. They had talked about getting married. He was trying to get into the longshoreman union. He had been a good dad to the kids, but then he was in the wrong place at the wrong time. Getting a dozen donuts right when somebody decided to rob the place. Things might have been different. But now this was her big chance, and she was gonna make the best of it. G-rated language. Oh, and she had to remind herself, don't say Whitey House. She'd been thinking that every time one of these white guys opened their mouths and she had to tell herself to knock it off so she didn't say it. But it was The Whitey House. Turn that off. Don't say it. What if someone asked about reparations? What should she say? Don't make any promises. That was the bottom line. She had to turn off her own feelings, but it was temporary.

It was time for her to step into the room and be a big hit. Strawberry Hair led her in, and there were mostly black and brown women in the audience, a few men and some members of the press. Strawberry Hair motioned for Kennedy to begin. Kennedy braced herself at the podium. Strawberry Hair pointed at her smile. Kennedy smiled then stretched out her arm, just like she had practiced and said, "Welcome to The Whitey House."

Junior sat at his desk, playing with his desktop Zen garden, a little square foot of sand with a few rocks, an air plant, and a rake. He raked a little sand, moved a rock, then moved the rock back. Chet walked through the door. Junior said, "Good morning, Chetsky. So! Kennedy tells me you're gay!" Chet was annoyed but decided to make the best of it. "Yes, Junior. I am."

Junior said, "I can't believe it! I'm shocked! I'm appalled. I'm mortified. What does that mean, anyway?"

Chet said, "It means I like men, Junior."

Junior said, "Oh! I thought it might be contagious." The worry made his voice quaver. "It's not contagious, is it?"

Chet said, "No."

There was an uncomfortable silence. Junior raked some sand, then Kennedy entered. She dropped some papers on Junior's desk. "Here's the papers you asked for."

Chet gave her a dirty look and walked out.

Kennedy shrugged and shook her head. "What's wrong with him?

Junior said, "Beats me."

Kennedy looked at the Zen garden. "What's that?"

"It's a Zen garden. The subtle movements of the sand, the rocks, the beauty, it's a stress buster."

Kennedy raised an eyebrow. "Whatever."

"Yeah, seems to just be raising my stress." Junior picked up the phone. "Kelly, this is the president. Yes. Yes, it is important this time. I want my Zen garden paved with concrete. Yes. Immediately. Thanks, you're a doll." He smiled at Kennedy. "You can't say J. Junior doesn't make a decision and act on it. So, how was your date with Chetsky? I mean, aside from the gay thing."

"I just had my first listening session!"

"How did it go?"

"Oh... pretty good." Kennedy nodded to the papers. "Those papers. It's the Middle East thing."

"Again?"

"I think this is a new one."

Junior mumbled under his breath. "I want to do a good job. But all these problems look the same!"

"Junior, they're talking nuclear war."

"Nuclear war? Man, what should I do?"

"I dunno, but we gotta solve this," Kennedy said.

"I'll need your help."

"I'm ready!"

"You're ready? Caroline's never ready. Does this mean you're interested in me?"

Kennedy moved closer to Junior. "Well, you're kinda cute." She stopped. What was she doing? She wanted to show everyone she could do this work. She didn't want to get involved with Junior! Yuck.

"What? The world's on the brink of nuclear war, and you want to tell me I'm cute? I kinda like that."

"Forget it," Kennedy said. She hesitated. "I want to be professional. It's just,

I get lonely. I'm only twenty-three. I want to be with someone."

Junior said, "You're with me... and Caroline. And Chet."

Kennedy said, "I mean a man. Someone to be with."

Junior said, "Do you mean a boyfriend?"

Kennedy said, "No, I mean a lover." She spread her hand wide, shoved it between his legs and took a hard grab.

Junior squealed, "Hee-yiiieee! Okay, you're right. This is how to deal with a nuclear war! Grab 'em by the balls!"

Kennedy said, "Kaboom."

Junior said, "That felt almost as good as a hole in one."

She pushed Junior on the desk and climbed on top of him. What was she doing? She needed to stop. Keep her distance from her boss. He would totally have a reason to get rid of her. Stop. Yes, she would stop. Junior said, "I can guess why they call you Kennedy."

"I...sorry. I just want to do a good job. I didn't mean to grab you. Let's forget this ever happened."

"I don't want to forget it. I liked it. But...."

"What?"

"My wife."

"You love her, and you can't do this?
"It's not that. If I do this, she'll beat living the hell out of me!"

Tip Murphy thumbed through a Hollywood star coffee book. Mae West. Maybe. Had she been a man? Jamie Lee Curtis. Nah. But was she a man? Mr. Rogers. Was he really a Navy SEAL sniper? What about Elvis? Already too many impersonators. Gloria Swanson... now she, she was distinguished. Norma, Norma Desmond... that was good pulp... Norma Desmond, that was right up his multiple personalities alley... but how about Norman. Norman Desmond... Norman, her great-great grandson. That was a good one. He'd start working on it.

Junior plugged in an automatic putting machine. He took a ball and a club and lined up his shot. He tapped the ball and missed by a mile. Junior said, "Just one more... just one more hole in one, then I'm gonna get on that Middle East crisis thing."

Fletcher Worthy stomped around the Oval Office, an unlit cigar in hand. "Did you hear what she did? Did you? What she did this morning?"

"Yes."

"She called The White House The Whitey House. In front of everyone. Television!"

"Oh! I thought you were gonna say she grabbed my balls."

"What? What are you doing, boy?" Fletcher took a swing at Junior's head. "This is the third and final time I'm telling you, you got to get rid of that girl! Then concentrate on trying to get re-elected! It's just like I always told you, Junior, women are trouble. That's why you pay for it and leave 'em!"

Junior said, "It's something more than that, Dad."

Fletcher said, "What the hell are you talking about?"

Junior said, "Caroline and I haven't been... well, things haven't been the best between us, and... I think I'm falling in love with the girl, Dad."

Fletcher threw the unlit cigar in the trash. "You're not in love with her! Did you get her pregnant, Junior? Don't do this to me again, I'm trying to be pro-life!"

Junior said, "I can't help it, Dad, I've had to throw convention to the wind, and, damn it all, I'm glad! After all, I'm the president, and I can be in love with her if I want."

Fletcher said, "I don't know why I ever adopted you. I shoulda taken you back to the orphanage that first week."

Junior said, "I wasn't in an orphanage. Your army buddy told you to take me."

"What are you thinking? If you're thinking! Listen. You're the president, and

187

that's exactly why you can't be in love with this girl. Or any girl, except that dried up prune of a wife of yours. I'm going to handle this, Junior. You may throw convention to the wind; guess where the convention will throw you! I'll send the girl back to where she came from. And don't worry, your old Dad will give her some money. Then you and I are having a long talk!"

Junior positioned the ball right at the mouth of the machine then rolled in a hole in one. "Okay, just one more. Just one more hole in one, then I'm really gonna deal with the Middle East."

Kennedy entered.

Junior said, "Kennedy, there you are. We were just talking about you. Can you believe this crazy crisis?"

Kennedy said, "Yeah, and it's about to blow up. And I mean with a big kaboom."

"Hey, did you call this place The Whitey House?"

"That just... kind of slipped out. Everything else went great."

Junior said, "What's the name of those countries again?"

Kennedy said, "I dunno. I think one starts with an I... or wait... an S. Maybe a P? But they want to blow each other to smithereens."

Junior said, "Oh well, whatever they're called. It's up to the old U.S. of A to get in there and uh, you know, do something. I'll solve this Middle East mess and then everyone will love me!"

Fletcher said, "Son, there are days I'm concerned I voted for you. Since when is this girl your Secretary of State?"

"She isn't," he said.

"Then she shouldn't be making decisions."

"Ah, she was just helping me, Dad."

"Excuse me," Kennedy said. "I'm still here."

Not for long, thought Fletcher Worthy.

It could not be that bad.

As the Middle East crisis began to escalate, Butts had heard rumors that the administration didn't even know which countries were involved. It could not be that bad. Hopefully.

Butts walked to the White House. He stopped and looked at the dome. It was almost fully repaired. He remembered that day the snow globe crashed down and broke into a million pieces. They had just buried Randall. It was the beginning of fall but unnaturally hot. Everything from those days was a blur—from Bessie going into labor, the rush to the hospital, the waiting room— fathers weren't in the delivery room then—to the birth that turned out to be a stillbirth. Rapidly planning then holding the funeral, and he had been exhausted, but his priority was Bessie. His goal was to take care of her.

He couldn't even remember what he had been doing, but he'd nudged the snow globe—he had kept it all those years, and it sat on the fireplace mantle—his elbow had barely tapped it, and it fell to the brick base of the fireplace and shattered. It shattered, just like Bessie's world had shattered. Just like his life had shattered. The water, the glass, the little White House, the bits of snow strewn across the floor. But it was only a toy. He didn't think "Rosebud" as it fell. *Randall* he thought. Randall, his boy who would never grow old. Randall.

The baby was in the grave next to Bessie, the grave where one day his coffin would be added. Butts had always been full of energy, but, recently, he had felt himself slow down, and it was hard to decide if it was worth carrying on as his daily aches and pains began to mount. But he had a mission. And he would continue as long as he could contribute to it.

The snow globe smashing to bits was like Citizen Kane when Kane said Rosebud and the globe rolled from his aged hand, met the floor, and disintegrated. Rosebud. No one could ever figure out what it meant, and at the end of the movie, it was Kane's sled, Rosebud. The irony, lost youth, lost innocence, lost dreams. As an adult, he had learned that Rosebud had been William Randolph Hearst's nickname for his mistress, Marion Davies', private place.

Rosebud. Some people have a whole lot of spare time on their hands to be naming the private parts of their mistresses.

And here he was. Tired, stiff, and cold, but determined to do something. Well, his great-grandfather hadn't been bound in slavery for Jedidiah to watch this country move from a great mountain to an avalanche and collapse into useless rubble. He had to do something. True, Junior's capabilities were limited, but that needn't matter. There were plenty of top-notch advisors who could guide him. Even if Junior couldn't be effective, they could. He just needed the right guidance.

He went through security clearance and up to the secretary. He could have called, but this was important. He needed to help Junior restore the truth of this office. Butts walked up to the secretary. "I need to speak with the president."

She looked at him. "Yes, Congressman Butts."

She disappeared briefly then reappeared. I'm afraid the president's not in today. Would you like to set up an appointment?"

Delayed but not defeated. Butts said, "Yes."

"Oh, it seems the president's schedule is pretty booked right now. How about next month?"

"That's too late!"

"Why don't I put you on the list, and if anything opens up, I'll call you."

"All right," said Butts, and he turned for the door. Butts left, then realized he had briefs to drop off. He returned and walked by the Oval Office, and as he did, the door closed. And just as that last sliver of a crack remained before the door fully shut, he saw Junior inside. Their eyes met. Butts felt his lips slightly drop open, then he walked on.

Chapter 18

Kennedy had intended to jog around the park. She'd put on sweats and running shoes, but as soon as she got there, she gave up on the jogging and started to walk. She'd called in sick. Nobody would look for her here. Those people were all glued to their desks. The job was a lot of stress—she didn't need stress from exercising. She needed this calm, this step after step after step. A chance to look at the trees and the flowers and the other people without the baby or Junior or Chet. There were beautiful roses. Pink ones and orange and yellow. She wished she'd had the time to learn the real names of roses or learn about painting or computers, or anything. She smelled the yellow rose, and the scent exploded in her nose like the cool rush of sherbet. She worried about Mom. Was she okay? And the twins, LaJames and

LaJohnny. They were big enough to keep themselves occupied. Things weren't going well here. She'd be back in San Francisco soon enough.

So, caught up in the worry of her mom and the perfume of the rose, she hadn't even seen him walk up.

"Hi. Beautiful, aren't they?"

"Yeah."

"Lady Hillingdon," he said.

"No, my name's Kennedy."

He laughed. "That's the name of the flower."

Oh great, another gay black man, she thought. "How'd you know that?"

"I used to work for the city parks."

"Oh, well, what do you do now?"

"I'm a DCPD."

She stopped and looked at him. He didn't have the best face on him, but he had some muscle. He wore a t-shirt, and his biceps were ripping it up. He had a shaved head—pure, solid, round, like a bald baby's head. He wore jeans, and she could see his quad muscles were barely held in by his jeans. He wasn't much to look at, but hey, he was 100% man. Growing up, cops had been the wrong side of the law. She imagined him like the men she'd seen on the tv show COPS. Scaling a fence with a flashlight in hand, he could cuff her to the bed and tell her she had the right to remain silent....

"What's your name?"

"Derrick. Want to get a cup of coffee?"
"Sure," she said.

Wanda sat at her kitchen table. Like most of her friends, she had a small, utility apartment in Washington D.C. The difference was, most of them had homes to return to and this was her home. It was small. A studio. The main room had her bed, TV, a small desk. There was a small kitchen and a bathroom. She could hide the kitchen when she wanted with a vinyl pocket door. She'd moved in seven years ago—confident it would be a short-term stay.

Her husband, Kevin, had taught at American University, poly sci. He was brilliant but hotheaded. He would say passionate. He'd been passed over for the department head position and abruptly walked off the job one day in anger. She had been applying for research projects, but after he quit, she'd had to get a job. She had to get work immediately, and to her shame, she'd taken a retail job. The joke had been, she was in young men's pants. Yeah, she'd gotten a big laugh out of that when she thought of all her student loans. Her husband was unemployed for three months, then was diagnosed with colon cancer. They hadn't cobraed his insurance, couldn't afford it at the time. Stage four colon cancer and no insurance, and after the diagnosis, they couldn't get insurance. He'd died within a year, and his death wiped out what little savings they'd had. As he was dying, he'd become more and more verbally abusive to her, and she found herself wishing him dead. Not long after his death she'd landed the job with Anderson, Anderson & Jacobs, it had seemed an ideal way to use her research and analysis skills, but aside from the health benefits, this job was about as rewarding as selling young men's pants.

The work didn't matter. A job was a job. It was what she wanted to do. Research. But this convenience apartment was driving her crazy. In high school, she had fantasized about getting married, having lots of kids, and living on a big farm. It took every cell in her body to keep from feeling bitter. Kevin had been a good husband... at first. It seemed like a different life—he, the gifted university professor, she the competent researcher. He didn't want kids, but maybe, over time, she could change his mind. She had felt lucky to snag him. She knew she was plain. A mousy brunette who kept her four eyes in a book. Tip always said she looked like a librarian. She was lucky to marry Kevin. Then the bad things happened, and almost as quickly as she had met and married him, he was gone from her life. After about a year, she'd met Tip. His ex-wife had suffered from depression and killed their two children then herself. Maybe that's where he learned some of his tricks. Tip never talked about his wife. Never even mentioned her. He had a similar apartment, at least he had a one bedroom, but to him, it was a blessing. Little to clean and no room to entertain. She'd thought maybe they would be living together by now or be married. Maybe they could get a little house in the mountains. Was she crazy or pathetic? Neither, really. She was just alone.

Kennedy pushed her cart through the huge aisles. She loved Costco. And, for the first time in her life, she could buy almost anything she wanted. Anything from Costco! It was a dream come true. Back in The City, she had to borrow her cousin's card, then she had to watch every penny because the stuff added up fast. But it was the cheapest place for baby diapers and the stuff the kids loved. Sometimes she would swap out her SNAP card two-to-one so she could get some cash and go to Smart and Final, but Costco! Costco was the bomb! Now, in DC, she had a check, and it was a big check! She could get snacks, meat, clothes—she could even buy water! She always drank it from the tap, but now she could buy it in a bottle! And she had a car—it was a rental car for now—but she had a car to put the groceries in! Didn't have to catch the bus or walk. Her cart was filled to the brim with snacks, and she was going to mail some Rice Krispies squares and pepperoni sticks to the boys. She was going to save up some money and buy her mom something nice. What would she like? A nice, new TV. A giant one.

She wheeled her cart and waited in line. There was a long line, but the wait was worth the savings. She pushed her load to the door. She hated that Costco checked her receipt. They said it was to make sure you'd "received all your items" but it was really to see if you'd ripped off anything. This act always made her feel ashamed. Because there'd been times when she really needed to steal some things, though she never did. At least they didn't just search the black folks. Still, it always felt wrong, and she kept her head down. There had been five carts in front of her, and within a few minutes, it was her turn. She held up her receipt, trying not to make eye contact, but then looked up.

"Derrick?" She was shocked to see Derrick, the same Derrick from the park, DCPD Derrick, standing at the warehouse door, Costco badge pinned to his shirt.

"Uh... Kennedy!"

"DCPD. Huh!" She pushed her cart through.

That was it. Men lied to her. Men were playas. Men were men! She loaded up her car, then fired it up. Men were stupid liars, saying they were DC cops when really, they were receipt checkers at Costco. Some white guy in a BMW swerved around, nearly hitting her. "White male privilege!" she yelled. That's what that was. She hated men for acting like they were better than everyone else, just seeing things and taking them and never thinking about anybody else. Then the thought hit her. "I'm gonna exercise MY white male privilege!" She pulled her car through the lot like a total asshole. She was gonna find that guy in the BMW, ride up on his bumper, then slam on her brakes right before she hit him. White male privilege. Bastards acting like the world owed them. That settled it. From now on, she was going to activate that part of her brain. She was going to think—What stupid, ignorant thing would a white guy do? And that's what she would do. She pulled out without looking. She didn't signal and pulled onto the freeway onramp. She knew what she wanted next.

Caroline's mother, Anne, had been a Miss Tennessee. Caroline had grown up surrounded by an onslaught of trophies, ribbons, and sashes. Every wall was stacked with pictures of her mother in pageants from age three until the Miss USA pageant, which had been rigged. Apparently one of the judges owed a very large favor to Miss Georgia's family. Anne should have won and came in second. And though Anne prayed daily for the newly crowned Miss USA to have to step down, due to family issues or health problems, or perhaps she could just die in a fiery car crash, but it never came to be, and for eternity, she was First Runner-Up. And every day, it gnawed a little more inside her.

No matter where Caroline stepped in the house, she was shadowed by her mother, Anne, with the perfectly coiffed hair, the flawless makeup, and endless pictures of her mother in tiara and gown. From birth, her mother had transferred her desire to Caroline. But Caroline would not be a First Runner-Up, no sirree bob. Nothing less than the full crown. And Caroline had been the dutiful daughter. She had glued on the permanent smile, learned baton twirling until she had callouses like flat little grapes on both hands, watched her figure in an almost unhealthy way. She was competitive. Her mother told her she was a late bloomer, that's all, and that none of the little pageants mattered. The only one that counted for anything was the Rutherford County Little Miss. Almost every girl who had won that had gone on to be Miss Tennessee.

Not a single day went by without her thinking about it, processing it, ruminating it to death. The Rutherford County Little Miss. She had practiced daily and was coached in every area. When the pageant came, she had done well in every category, the casual wear, the formal wear, the speech, then came her best event, the talent competition. She had a tap dance routine, with the baton, to "This Is My Country." She had new, patent leather tap shoes. She wore a stars and stripes leotard with glistening rhinestones. Her hair was pulled back in a French twist, and her makeup was flawless. She stepped out, massive smile on her face. The music started. She took her first step–right. She was about to ball-heel-ball-heel-shuffle-shuffle-paradiddle-paradiddle, and she took that first step–right, and her leg slipped out from under her, and she fell on her ass. She jumped back up and finished the routine, but she had fallen on her ass! All the practice. All the coaching. All the planning. And she fell on her ass. And that was that. If she couldn't win The Rutherford County Little Miss, she wouldn't be Miss Tennessee. She couldn't be Miss USA. She hadn't matched her mother. She would always be Second Lady. All of her events had been stellar, and she fell on her ass! Every damn thing else in that pageant went off flawlessly. Flawlessly! She came in 2nd place. Second! The worst place. Runner-Up. All because she fell on her ass! She felt like she fell on her ass every day after, for her entire life.

Her mother, Anne, had married well. Monty Beauregard, fourth generation in the South. His grandfather had been a senator, his father had been a judge. Caroline had an older brother who had been groomed to be the next Senator Beauregard. Everett volunteered for the military and though his father intervened, tried to get him out, then got him an easy post, Everett became obsessed with guns, the rifle range, target practice. Without experiencing the torment suffered by many in military combat, Everett Beauregard developed a fondness for killing. While he might have made a career of the military, even the army found his love for blood distasteful and processed him for a Section 8. Two days before his discharge, he ran, never to be heard from again. His AWOL stint resulted in a dishonorable discharge in absentia, and the whole fiasco broke his father. Montgomery had always loved a cocktail or two. After Everett's disappearance, he tried to drown his sorrows in alcohol, and ended up going for a long, endless swim. Anne had hired several investigators to find her son, but he left no trail. She had to assume the worst and closed the door on that part of her life.

Caroline had always hated Everett. He was valued more than she was, and the only bad feelings she had about his disappearance was the guilt of being happy that he was presumed dead. Caroline decided she would become the next Senator Beauregard. Her father spent most nights passed out on the rug in front of the console TV. Her mother started a charity for military veterans with mental health issues, but after she met a few of them, they all just seemed so troubled, she gave it up. She encouraged Caroline's studies, pointing out that it was one way to get a man. Caroline met Junior in college. She helped him pass every class, and she was the one who had finally passed the bar for him, dressing in one of his suits. As a reward for her efforts, his daddy arranged their marriage. She ditched her thoughts of becoming a senator and decided she'd make her mark as a politician's wife... not just any politician's wife. She had her eye on the biggest plum of them all—the president's wife. And now she'd arrived and for what end? To be humiliated by her imbecile of a husband! And the little whore trying to get into his pants! They would both pay dearly for this. Dearly, dearly, dearly.

She couldn't be with a married man. She'd been with lots of guys, but she wasn't a ho. And it was wrong. It was one of the Ten Commandments. Wasn't it? Thou shalt not be a ho.... Yeah, it was one of the commandments, maybe it was number eight. Then again, she'd lied, and broken some of the other ones, and all she had to do was ask forgiveness. And if it made her feel better, if it helped the country, was it really a sin? Junior was always saying his marriage was as good as over. She didn't want people to just think she was a black girl who was good in bed—though she did like the idea that they knew she was good in bed—but they needed to know she had a brain, too. She still needed to show these White House fools that she was valuable. There were all sorts of white guys who hadn't gone to college. And they thought they knew everything, and because they acted like they knew everything, doors opened for them. She needed to do the same thing. She didn't need college, money, a prominent family. She needed confidence.

Kennedy walked into Junior's office. She remembered her new motto was "What Would Whitey Do?" Whitey would be a ho. She was only twenty-three. She wanted sex, dammit. And the white guys, they just barged in places and demanded what they wanted. She shut the door.

"You don't need to shut the door."

"Yes, I do."

Junior was worried. The only time anyone shut the door was when he had done something wrong. "Am I in trouble?"

"No, but you're going to be." She walked over to him. She slid her hands on the outside of his thighs, starting from the knee, then slid up to his ass. She started to massage his butt.

"You know, um, careful of the ol' presidential pooper there!"

She shoved him on the desk, then wrapped her leg around his thigh. She rubbed her thigh against his, up and down, her hips gyrating harder and harder.

Junior felt like he was going to pass out. He'd begged and whimpered to Caroline for sex, and he'd gone without for the last three months. He hadn't had a woman throw herself at him since... well, since the other time Kennedy threw him on the desk, but they hadn't done it then. Only made out until his Daddy walked in. His brain was about to short circuit. He had to make a choice. Little Junior was already starting to stand to attention.

Kennedy started to unbutton her boring, navy-blue blouse. Underneath, she had on a sexy, black bra. *Man, she's got some chimichangas!* thought Junior. Forget Caroline's standard 32B issue, he was right! Kennedy must have been a 40 DD at least! Maybe a DDD. Should he stop? He knew he needed to make a choice soon. Kennedy cupped her big breasts into her hands and pushed them up. Then she took out her soft tongue and ran it across her right boob. "You licked your own tittie! Caroline will barely let me touch hers with my hands!"

Kennedy slowly ran her tongue from one end of her upper lip to the other. "Listen to me, Junior. You're going to fuck me. And you're going to fuck me hard. You're going to fuck me good. You're going to fuck me until you scream for your mama."

Junior's brow wrinkled. "I think I need an index card to write all this down."

Her mouth was still slightly open. Her eyes pierced into him. Should he do what was right? Stay faithful to his wife, do what the good book said, protect his country? Or, should he run his tongue on that big bodacious tittie? Kennedy dropped her embrace on him. Maybe it was over. Maybe she'd changed her mind. Maybe it had just been a test.

Kennedy reached behind her and undid the clasps of the bra. She held it in the air for a moment then dropped the bra to the ground. Nipples! Round, fat, little bullseyes! There was no decision to make! His mouth zeroed in and lobbed on to the right nipple.

"Oh!" she said. "Don't bite so hard!"

As the vice president, Tip Murphy was in charge of the Senate, and though he was rarely called in, today, he would be needed to break a tie vote. He tapped the gavel and realized he didn't know what to say. "This session... is now in session!" Finally, the respect he deserved. It was a full house, and all eyes were on him.

"Who are you today? Fang?" shouted one senator.

"We want Blanche! We want Blanche!" a small group cheered.

"Where's Ramona?"

"Don't let Lightning Rod near the curtains!"

Fools! Didn't they understand his ploy? Couldn't they see that beneath the veneer he was the most qualified politician to run the Senate?

"Come on! Who are you today?" The mood was just giddy, hoping he'd show up as one of his personas.

"I'm Tip. Tip Murphy."

There was rustling in the seats. Some people looked discouraged and started to pack up their briefs. Tip ran his tongue on the inside of his cheek. He felt a canker sore.

"I'm Tip. Tip! Tip-Aroooo!" he howled to the ceiling. Senators started emptying their briefs and sat up to attention. Tip barked for twenty seconds then said, "Now, let's get down to business. Arf!"

This time, it would have to work. There was no other option. He had considered several methods. Another shooting attempt, poison darts, running him down with a car. From there, his thoughts dwindled to the sheer nutty, including catapulting an anvil into Junior the same way Wile E. Coyote did to the Roadrunner. He searched the Internet, studied *The Art of War,* watched *The Sopranos.*

Finally, he had hit on an idea worthy of Roald Dahl. He got a bunch of bananas, then he froze them all. Then, with a paring knife, he whittled each banana to a sharp point, then froze them again. He would come up on Junior, stab him to death with a frozen banana shiv, then by the time anyone investigated, the banana would be thawed out and never recognized as the weapon.

He had plotted the times precisely. Junior would arrive for a short ceremony in the Rose Garden at noon. At noon exactly, Junior walked out. Secret Service were everywhere. There was no way he could get close to him—what was he thinking? He reached into his pocket. The bananas had thawed—maybe from his body heat?—and they had turned to mush. Stupid, stupid, stupid. What was he thinking? There would be no death by banana. There would be no death by any fruit. He realized the stress, the demands, the failures—he couldn't even think straight. He wasn't killing anyone with a banana! Fat Ass collapsed into one of the folding chairs that had been placed for the ceremony. Fat Ass leaned back on his fat ass. He had failed. And that meant only one thing.

Chapter 19

She'd studied. She'd prepared. She was ready. For the past week, she'd poured over the press clippings, demanded old television and film footage of all her events, had consulted with several designers, and today would be the fruition. Jacqueline Bouvier Kennedy. Caroline had decided to use her maiden name as well. Caroline Beauregard Worthy. It had a ring. She'd tried ten different outfits and finally settled on a Halston suit. It was beige. It had a classic look, and that's what she was going for. To mimic, nay, to surpass Jacqueline Bouvier Kennedy at the class game. She toyed with a pillbox hat, but it was too early. She'd save that for later. Then she'd practiced with every aide she could corner—she'd practiced the tour with the vigilance of a manic docent.

She could answer ANY question that came up. This would be her most brilliant hour!

And it would be with Barbara Walters. Could there be a more glorious event in Caroline's life? Yes, she'd fantasized being interviewed, sitting at tea, giving the White House tour, but it had always been with a nameless, faceless reporter. Not Barbara Walters! Caroline smiled, and it was as if sunshine rolled up her body, from the toes to the forehead. She was happy. "Barrett!" she yelled. "I need more Botox!"

Her smile was carved deep in her face, like a scary jack-o-lantern. She stood at the White House entrance as if she opened the door for any guest. Barbara Walters greeted and entered, then they stopped for a hair and makeup check and had Barbara greet and enter again.

They sat on a loveseat. Caroline poured Barbara a cup of tea, just as she'd practiced. "Caroline, did you ever expect to be the First Lady?"

"Me?" she offered up her well-rehearsed laugh. "Barbara, never in my wildest dreams would I have EVER thought little ol' me would be the wife of the president!" What a lie that was. She'd dreamed it every night. That and more. First Lady... that was only the beginning of her dreams. She smiled, but this one wasn't faked. She smiled thinking of her dreams to come.

Caroline had shown the Oval Office, the family dining room, and the Press Room. The tour had moved as smooth as a case of ex-lax. Her practice had paid off. She could easily rattle statistics on renovations, rumors, and historical fact. She shared another one. "Yes, well, the White House was designed by Irish-born architect, James Hoban. In 1702, he won a competition to design the structure."

Barbara said, "I never realized you were such a historian!"

Caroline put on her serious face. "I think it's important for all of us Americans to know, and be proud of, our history."

Only one stop left. The Lincoln bedroom. And this would be fast—certainly no more than five minutes, probably less. There wasn't much to see, but Barbara wanted to use it to discuss Bill Clinton's legacy.

"Unfortunately, some of President Clinton's actions left this country with a few black eyes. As a matter of fact, it looked like Hillary might have been responsible for at least one of them."

Caroline threw the door open, and there he was. President Jackass. Junior was humping and bumping Kennedy on the bed. Caroline froze. Her mind went blank. All the planning. But she hadn't planned for this.

She had told him to stay out. Junior kept humping and bumping, his ass pumping up and down.

Barbara Walters' face was frozen too. "My," she said. That was it. The cameraman was all over it.

Caroline kicked Junior with the force of a Sherman tank. "What do you think you're doing?"

"Uh... listening to the voice of the people?"

"Why are you..." She wasn't sure what word to use as the cameras were live... "intercoursing this girl?"

"Because you wouldn't do it with me!"

Kennedy grabbed a sheet, wrapped it around her, and ran for the door. She saw the camera and yelled, "Oh shit!"

Caroline grabbed Barbara's mic and started beating Junior with it. Still nude, he ran around the room trying to dodge the blows. Caroline crumpled into a heap on the floor. She wiped away tears and saw her mascara had smeared everywhere. She waved the cameras away then remembered she'd seen a picture where Jackie O's mascara had smeared too. She tried to strike that pose.

Donaldson and Fat Ass watched a fiberglass log zoom down the flume, hit the deep water, and drench the log riders. They were at a theme park, open winter weekends. It hadn't been Fat Ass's choice.

"Okay, so it didn't work. Maybe you should've sat on him!"

"Har-de-har-har. Trust me. This new idea. It'll work. Foolproof. I can do this."

"I've already trusted you. It's gotten me nowhere."

They both stood there for a moment, but it felt like hours passed. They stared out at the log ride, group after group getting soaked, screaming, as if they didn't anticipate their fate.

"Let's go for a walk," Donaldson said. That was pretty neutral. They walked together through the park. Donaldson in a suit, out of place, Fat Ass in khakis and a polo. Finally, Donaldson said, "Let's ride the roller coaster." Well, that was that. It was the kiss of death, except it was a roller coaster. They both moved from the uneven planks to concrete and plodded along toward the coaster.

It hadn't been a good morning, but a call from Mom always cheered her up.

"I saw you on TV."

"You did? Did I look good?"

"You looked fine!" Kennedy could always count on Mom to be supportive. Then Mom said, "Except you need to get some damn clothes on."

"Listen, Mom. It's complicated."

213

"I told you not to go there. Now, I would never say anything bad about my daughter." She had that drawl to her voice. "But a woman who sleeps with another woman's man. I would say she is a b-i-t-c-h."

"You don't have to spell it, Mom. It's not what you think. I'm working for the president."

Then with more bite, she said, "Oh. Is that what the president hired you for?"

Without a goodbye, Kennedy hung up the phone.

They stood in line for eight minutes. Fat Ass thought about running away. That would just delay the inevitable. They took a few steps closer. How was any of this going to happen anyway? Maybe he was wrong, fooling himself, it was all a ruse, a big scare, and tomorrow would arrive, and he would come up with a new way to kill Junior.

He knew he couldn't fit in the seat. What would they do? Fat Ass looked down the line at some of the park's other offerings. The thing that kept catching his eye was a fair food alley that included a stand that sold deep-fried Twinkies. He'd walked by it twice, as if he wasn't interested, and kept thinking of ways to get one, or two, without looking like a fat, greedy slob. He wanted one. But he was trying to eat better, so he passed it by. But what if this turned out to be his last day on Planet Earth? What if that had been his last chance to eat a deep-fried Twinkie? He should have had one. Then they were at the front of the line, and the ride operator made them wait until an empty car pulled in. No one said anything to him, that he was too large, or the bar wouldn't fit, or anything. The cars pulled up, and Fat Ass headed for the car in front of him, third car down.

"Front car," the ride operator said, and he motioned his arm to the front, leading the way to his demise. Fat Ass moved to the front car. The ride operator lowered the safety bar as far as he could, then he latched it up, in an odd way. "Enjoy the ride, sir." Fat Ass read the ride operator's name badge. Timmy.

Donaldson headed for the second car and spoke to Timmy. "I have a back injury. Slipped disk."

"I'm afraid you can't ride."

"That's too bad. Could you make an exception, just this once?"

"Sorry, sir. Liability."

"I guess I'll just watch from here." Donaldson stepped to the side as the cars filled up.

"No, wait! I have a back injury too!" Fat Ass tried to get out, but it was impossible, and Donaldson waved goodbye to Fat Ass as the cars chug, chug, chugged up the incline, the chain cranking the train up.

Fat Ass leaned back in the car. He filled almost the entire seat. It was embarrassing. He took up an entire row, a row that could fit three kids or two adults. Every jerk of the chain pulled him closer. The sun was out and was exceptionally bright for winter, and with every yank of the car, Fat Ass felt a jolt in his eyes, like the light that comes with a migraine. Then the car hit the top of the arc and released. He felt himself gliding on the track. He hadn't been on a roller coaster since he was in the sixth grade. The car bulleted down the steep incline, his hair zipping in the wind. Maybe this wasn't it. Maybe this was the prelude, the foreplay, the torture of guessing. Maybe Donaldson really did have a back injury. Maybe Donaldson would change his mind and realize that the new idea would work, and he only needed one more chance. Maybe he just needed some firmer bananas. It was all okay. He had been foolish. Donaldson wasn't going to kill him. Certainly not in front of all these children. There was no need to bump him off. Fat Ass leaned back in the car, and for the first time that morning, breathed a complete chest of air. He didn't have to worry. He was safe. Enjoy the ride, sir.

The car traveled another incline and approached the corkscrew. The steel car was picking up speed. It was actually fun. He was going to enjoy this. Fat Ass yelled for the hell of it and held his arms up in the air. Right when he did, the safety bar gave, and as the car whipped down the first curve of the corkscrew, Fat Ass was catapulted into the blinding winter sky. For a moment, his ass blocked the sun, and viewed from just the right place, it was just like a partial eclipse. He had kept his arms in the air, but as he flew, they bent a bit, and his hands turned into claws. A look was on his face, but it was hard to tell if it was horror, enlightenment, or acceptance. He tried to breathe out, but the force was too great. Either from resignation or G-forces, his arms dropped to his side. He was a massive human torpedo, zinging along in a tall trajectory across the theme park skyline. His view was a racing blur, but colors! Colors everywhere. The height! He was flying. Light as a feather! The sound! Like the whistle of a Piccolo Pete at 4th of July. Then the sound started to arc. That meant one thing. He was no longer light. The laws of physics were kicking in, and the downward spiral was commencing. The blur was changing—hazy. Could he pick Donaldson from the crowd? No. Could he pick anything from the glazed fury? No. Then he did, he was able to make something out. It was the deep-fried Twinkie stand. He should have had one. That was his final thought.

Chapter 20

Okay, so she hadn't outclassed Jacquelyn Bouvier Kennedy Onassis. But she wouldn't be humiliated. She would make them both pay—and in a very public and a very painful way. She didn't know how or where or when. But both of them would pay. And in very different ways. How dare they! The crowning moment of her life, a tour with Barbara! How dare they humiliate her in front of the nation, in front of the world, in front of Barbara Walters! She felt exactly as she had when she fell on her ass—the rage, the embarrassment, the desire for revenge, burning like a Weber with a bucket of kerosene. They would not get away with this. She would have to exact the type of comeuppance that would make them feel the same humiliation she had experienced. She would take her time and do it right.

Murphy pulled the mascara wand up across his lashes. He'd used it a hundred times, but it was still a trial. Wanda sat on the bed. She pulled the threads from his comforter. "Would you stop that?" He said.

"Stop what?"

"Stop destroying my comforter."

Wanda sighed. "We need to talk," she said.

"It's nearly new, and you're going to pull every thread out of it."

"Okay. I'll stop touching your comforter."

He'd made her mad, and he'd done it on purpose. He figured he should back off. "Go ahead. I just want to put on a little more blush."

She stood up, holding on to a pillow. "This thing's gotten way out of hand."

"What thing?"

"This!" She motioned, waving her hands around his makeup and mirror.

Murphy said, "Oh, Wanda, you're just working too hard."

"I am not working too hard. But your phony multiple personalities act is putting me over the edge."

"This?" he asked motioning to his bra and panties set.

"You're going to get found out. And it'll ruin us both."

Murphy said, "Are you nuts? This is the best career move I've ever made."

Wanda's voice sounded as if she'd cry. "You've all but lost your identity."

Murphy said, "I know exactly what I'm doing. I can do whatever I want... and always blame it on someone else. Best of all, the public loves me. I can do no wrong."

"You're doing wrong every day!"

Murphy said in his Blanche voice, "Honey child, you just leave it to me. I'm gonna show ya'll how to turn a lil' white lie into legend."

Junior tried to make sense of the charts. "Okay, the whole getting caught on TV having sex thing has brought my approval rating down to a new low with conservatives. On the positive side, it's up with the Democrats! Erg. My neck is killing me! I had to sleep on the presidential sofa last night!"

"Well, what do you expect, son? You had the chance to be re-elected and you've blown it. You've blown it every single day."

"Chet, this is all your fault!"

"My fault? How is it my fault?"

"If you'd told me Barbara Walters was coming, I would've used the closet!"

"I did tell you."

"And Kennedy wouldn't even have been with me if you weren't gay! This is all your fault for being gay!"

Fletcher slid a step away from Chet.

"Gay means he likes boys, Dad."

"I know what gay means! We already had this discussion!" Fletcher threw his hat on the floor and started stomping around the room in his cowboy boots. He always acted like that when he had no idea what to do. Finally, he stopped and said, "We need a plan. Something to deflect the attention of this on to something else."

Junior said, "I know. Let's have a press conference and tell everyone Chet's gay. That should do it."

"I'd really prefer we not do that," Chet said.

"Then you better come up with something! What about the Middle East thing? What about a war, Dad?"

Chet closed his eyes as he spoke, "We are not starting a war."

"Quiet, you, you're gay. What would you know about war? What kind of war are you thinking, son?"

"Well, something that gets the heat off me."

"We are not starting a war because you got caught with your trousers down! War is not an option!"

"It's worked for every other president."

Donaldson sat on a park bench and flipped through the Post. There was the briefest mention of the accident at the park. A fatality at a local theme park resulted in the ride being closed until it could be inspected. Fat Ass had only ranked a paragraph, and no eyebrows were raised. Perfect. He'd already recruited another mercenary. He sat on the park bench near Donaldson, a ratty and distracted homeless man. Donaldson folded the Post, then looked over at him.

Donaldson guessed they were about the same age, but the homeless man looked grizzled from years of life on the street. He had on old sneakers, the right one had a hole near the toe and the tread was tearing off. He wore threadbare Levis that were at least two inches too long. They were covered in so much filth it looked as if he had wiped used engine oil up and down the legs. He wore several shirts—a ratty t-shirt, a filthy thermal, and a wool shirt. Donaldson could smell him from three feet away. Donaldson had smelled something like that before—sort of like a cross between a wet sheep and a corpse. The man had a frizzy unkempt beard, and his hair was matted like a lost poodle. Donaldson shook his head. How would this nutcase get past any security? Yet the homeless look might make him seem less of a threat. It might work in his favor, or maybe the Secret Service would give him a ten-foot berth cause this character smelled like shit dipped in grease.

"I'll kill that motherfucker for free. And his wife."

"I'll give you two hundred to get started. When it's wrapped up, there's ten thousand waiting for you." Donaldson pretended to yawn and raised his arms up over his head. He reached into the folds of the Post and pulled out eight twenties that had been carefully folded into a small inch-by-inch packet. Then he yawned again, and stretched his arms wide, slipping the money into the man's hand. "No mention of my name, of course. It's Tip Murphy. That's my name. And it can't be traced back to me, Tip Murphy."

"No problem, Tip Murphy," the man said.

"What shall I call you?" several thoughts clumped up in Donaldson's head—Dirtbag Dreadhead, Sir Washanot, Mr. Nasty. Before Donaldson could pull back, the homeless man grabbed his hand and shook it with a single, firm pulse. "Call me Everett," he said.

Kennedy leaned back on her couch, phone in one hand, drink in the other. She said, "Hey, Mom, how's it going?"

"When you coming home?"

"Look, Mom, all that mess. It was an accident. I'm here to help my country."

"I guess you help your country by spreadin' your legs."

Kennedy said, "I'm working, and I like it, Mom."

223

"Your babies miss you."

Kennedy said, "I miss them. Mom, I'm makin' good money. Enough for all of you to come out here and live with me."

"Oh no. Just because some crazy white boy's keepin' you shacked up there in the big fancy White House, I'm not gonna pick up and leave my home."

Kennedy said, "Mom, I want the best for the kids. I want them to go to a good school. I want them to get a chance at a good life."

"If you want that, then you oughta be home where you belong. I knew you'd turn out this way. No good."

Kennedy said, "Mom, I do nothing and I'm no good. I try and do something and I'm no good. Why can't I please you?"

"Cause you no damn good."

Kennedy said, "Bye, Mom. Tell everybody hi."

Of all the men she knew, which one would make Junior the angriest? No, that wasn't the way to approach this. She needed to pick the next in line for power. Then she would take down that twit of a husband, divorce him and marry the next in line for power, the next president. Then she'd still get to be First Lady. That was it. And that meant the vice president. Tip Murphy. Well, he was single. He did have that girlfriend, but she was obviously a lesbian. Would she have to marry all his personalities, or just one? That whole multiples act rang false to her. She'd known him for years and had only seen one personality—the one that drank and complained how life hadn't given him a fair shake. So, he was fat and ruddy, and he occasionally wore women's clothes. Oh well, it wasn't much worse than Junior. Hopefully, she could just wear gloves and give him the occasional hand job. She knew he frequented the Ballot Box with all the old cronies. It would be simple. She could put on her best—or, what if he was dressed as Blanche and Blanche's best was better than her best? Don't think about it, just go. Just go. She grabbed her handbag and had her driver take her to the tavern.

War. He wouldn't be the education president. He would be the war president. That would get their attention. Junior was walking the grounds when he saw Congressman Butts. "Hello, Congressman Butts."

"Hello, Jerry. How are things going?"

"Excellent. I've decided to start a war."

"That's not good news."

"It's great news. I can't lose. See, I have the indigo heart." Junior opened his coat to reveal the medal, a deep blue, almost black, heart mounted on a round, silver base.

"What did you win that for?" Butts asked.

"I didn't win it. It's my father's. My real father's. You know, I was adopted. My father was in the military. He threw himself on a grenade. He saved his entire troop—seventeen men. He sacrificed himself. He gave up his life. Dad—Fletcher Worthy—adopted me."

"Well, where was your biological mother? Why didn't she take care of you?" Butts asked.

"I... I don't know. I'll ask him." In all his forty-seven years, Junior had never thought about what had happened to his real mother. "I don't think she threw herself on a grenade."

"There's a lot to be learned from your real father," Butts said.

"It's the indigo heart."

Butts wasn't a military expert, but he hadn't heard of the indigo heart, but the medal didn't matter, the mettle did. He thought about saying that to Junior but knew it would take half the afternoon to explain it. "Your father sacrificed himself so others could live. He was fighting for freedom. We all need to follow his lead."

"Well, where would I go jump on a grenade? The Army-Navy store?"

"You don't have to jump on a grenade. You need to make choices that help others live—all people in the United States, all people in the world. This is why we have to prevent wars, not start them. We don't live in an isolated bubble. Everything we do as a country impacts every other country. Everything you do as a human being impacts every other human."

"You sure are smart, Congressman Butts. I wish I could ask you everything."

"You have two pieces of ammo."

"Oh yeah, the gun in my desk... what's the other one?"

"I meant the medal and the watch."

"I'd barely bruise anyone with those!"

"When you're in doubt, touch the medal. Your father is there. When you need answers, open the watch. I'll be there."

Junior had the watch. He took it out and opened it. Butts slapped his shoulder. "You have all the answers inside you. We all do." Slowly, Butts stood up and started to walk away. It was obvious he had arthritis and was stiff. Junior watched him take several steps.

"Congressmen Butts!" Butts turned and faced him. Junior held up the watch and clasped it shut. "Thanks for the watch." Butts smiled, gave one nod, and slowly walked on.

At the other end of the bar, she saw Donaldson. He leaned against the bar, one fist on one hip, the other elbow on the bar, drink in hand. He was looking right at her. He must have been watching her the entire time. She picked up her purse and headed for the door. He moved from the bar and headed straight for her. "Don't go. Why don't you have a drink with me."

"Because I can't stand you. That's one reason."

"Oh really? I find that unusual. We may have more in common than you think. For starters, a common enemy. Your husband."

"Maybe I will have that drink. But just one." She walked toward a table and felt her pantyhose chafe. She hadn't felt that odd sensation for years—when was the last time? The day she lost the Little Miss Rutherford County pageant.

The drinks arrived, and Donaldson picked his up and said, "Hello." He pursed his lips.

"Just what is it you want?" Caroline said.

He didn't answer immediately. He looked her up and down, as if she was naked, as if he was thinking about how to have her. "I was going to ask you the same thing, but with a different inflection."

"Listen. I don't need to be ridiculed."

"No. You don't." He took another sip of the top-shelf gin. "We want the same thing. Caroline." He added her name late.

"What's that?" she asked.

"Both of those punk bastards taken down a peg. I'm here to serve, Caroline. Just give me the word, and they're both toast." He slowly wiped his lips. She looked at him. Donaldson always moved like a shadow, day or night, indoors or out, he was like a chisel-cut silhouette creeping under a bright, full moon. What did he really want? She would never find out. And "toast"—did he mean "get them" or did he mean "kill them." Toast. They were toast.

What a delicious thought. A subservient lackey willing to follow her every whim. There was no justice. The only justice was the one she created. And even if there was justice, then screw justice, they'd humiliated her in front of the entire world!

But she had already decided. Toast wasn't enough. Let the little harlot be humiliated in front of the entire world. Let her see what it felt like. And Junior. She could take him down in an instant. But if he was dumped as president, then she wouldn't be First Lady... she'd be Runner-Up Lady. Forty-seven years she'd spent creating this persona, meticulously selecting the right hairstyle, the correct attire, the proper voice. She refused to let her two score and seven years go down the drain. Tip O'Neill was next in line. She had to get away from Donaldson and find Tip O'Neill. Where was he? He was always here. She had to find him. She had to marry him. And then she saw him.

Chapter 21

Caroline sauntered over to Murphy's table. "Mind if I join you?"

"Have a seat. I've never seen you in here before." He reached over and touched Caroline's hand.

Caroline said, "I wanted to... to talk politics."

Murphy said, "Right." He gave Caroline a big, boozy smile then said, "So, how's your love life?

Caroline said, "About as successful as his Presidency."

Murphy said, "Whoa! That bad, huh?"

He took a look at her. She was not his type. Her clothes were too conservative. He liked to see a little skin. Her hair and makeup were meticulous, he liked things a little rumpled. She was completely anal... his tastes ran a different direction. Still, she was female. And she was there. It's not like he was gonna marry her. She was just a conquest. One more pair of legs to part open. He slid his finger up her arm.

Murphy said, "It's just not right... A First Lady should be treated like royalty... pampered... spoiled... spanked!

Caroline said, "Spanked?"

Murphy said, "Junior's having an affair. With Kennedy. But of course, you already knew that."

Caroline flinched, then suppressed all emotion. She said, "Look, I have a... proposition."

"Proposition? I like the sound of that."

"I'm First Lady."

"I know."

"I'm a good First Lady."

"Not gonna argue with that."

"I want to stay First Lady."

"Okay..."

Inside Murphy's apartment, three people struggled under the sheets. Murphy screamed, "Oh dahlin', touch me theah agin! Your kiss is sweetah than mah-ma-lade!"

A body wrestled around, then popped up from the sheets. It was Kennedy. She said, "Oh no, I ain't makin' it with Blanche."

Murphy said, "That's okay. Cuz this is Rod! And I'm gonna hump you to death!"

Kennedy said, "Oh, I like Rod! Do me, Rod! Bang me all night!"

Caroline primly sat up from the sheets. While the other two were nude, she wore a red nightie. She looked at them. Sleeping with his mistress AND his vice president. That would show him. Then she would fire Kennedy. That would show them both.

Murphy said, "What about you, Caroline? Do you want to press the flesh with Rod?"

What should she say? She didn't want to press ANY flesh. But wait—there was one thing she wanted. Caroline said, "To be honest with you... I'm rather fond of... Fang!"

Wanda walked up to the door and took out her key. From inside, she could hear hellacious barking. When did Tip get a dog? Make that two dogs! And one sounded like a female in heat.

She walked in and followed the barking to the bedroom. The bedroom door was shut. Odd, as it was never shut. He must have bought two dogs and locked them in the bedroom. Wanda flung the door open to see Murphy, Kennedy, and two unknown legs making a not-quite-a-hero sandwich. Kennedy held on to a pair of female legs and Tip seemed to be humping the other girl from the rear, it was hard to tell. Doggy style? Really? It had to be doggy style? The whole scene made her sick. She thought they were committed. She was thinking more and more that he needed to be.

Murphy jumped out of bed. He said, "Wanda! It's not how it looks! It's not how it looks! Give me a chance to explain!"

She looked at him then said, "You dirty dog," and she walked out the door.

Murphy chased after Wanda. When the door slammed, Caroline slid upright. "She didn't see me, did she?"

"I thought you WANTED someone to see you!" Kennedy said. "That's why you set up the camera!"

Right, Caroline thought. She had forgotten about the camera. How else would this news get out? None of this had been pleasant, lying in bed with these two was as bad as Junior. She'd just turned her head off. Why was it she always did that? She looked at Kennedy lying next to her on her side. Her breasts were large, the lower one spread out against the bed sheet, the upper one rolling on to the lower. She looked at Kennedy's eyes, and for the first time in her life, Caroline realized she'd never really looked at anyone. She moved her hand toward Kennedy's breast. Kennedy took the hand and guided her. It was soft and round, and she moved her index finger to the nipple and rolled it around and around. Kennedy took Caroline's hand and slid it between her legs. Caroline's heart skipped. She'd never touched HERSELF there much less anyone else! She'd never played with her own breasts, and here she was in bed with the woman who'd cheated with her husband. Moments before when she'd been crawling around the sheets, she'd just pretended she was lost and hadn't done anything, and now her hand was touching the pubic hairs, feeling the moistness, working its way deeper.

Kennedy opened her mouth and kissed Caroline. Caroline's hand fell from between her legs and she embraced Kennedy. They made out for a minute, then Kennedy kissed Caroline's chin, her neck, her breastbone. What was she doing? She kissed her abdomen, her belly, then she slid her tongue from Caroline's bellybutton right into her secret garden! Caroline thought she would scream, but instead, a deep, sonorous moan came out. Murphy came back in then. He stood at the door, watching Kennedy go down on Caroline, and he got harder than he'd been in years. He walked over to Caroline and moved her so her back arched over the mattress. He held his dick to her lips. She wasn't going to do this! She was a good girl! Yet she pressed her mouth to the head of his penis and kissed it, then again and again. Then she went full force on the head of his dick, plunging her whole mouth around it. The only man she'd ever been with was Junior, and now she had a woman licking her kitten and a man thrusting his privates into her mouth. She turned on her side, and Kennedy moved with her. She held Murphy's cock in her hand and rolled her tongue around it, then licked the bottom of the head. She took the head in her mouth, and it popped out and slapped her in the cheek. What was she doing? She reached her arms and grabbed his legs. For the first time in her life, she let go. She relaxed her hips and could feel Kennedy lapping up her wetness, her mouth dropped, and Murphy was pumping his hips into her. They were in control of her. She'd never lost control before, and now she had. She had lost it completely. And she loved it.

Chapter 22

Caroline sat at the table. The cup of coffee in front of her had gone cold. She watched Junior and little Jeffrey fight over a breakfast cereal toy—a little boat powered by a balloon. Jeffrey drove the boat around the table past the butter dish, up the box of cereal, then around the bowl of fruit until Junior grabbed it out of his hand. Junior drove it over the chair back, up the cereal box, then across the table when Jeffrey grabbed it back. Caroline watched. Forty-seven years of this. Forty-seven times three-sixty-five times twenty-four times sixty times sixty... that would be the number of seconds she'd had to endure in this lifetime. She sat. The clock loudly clapped at the passing of each additional second. Another, another, another. Time didn't slip past, it built, one molecule of anger plus another plus another plus another until a personal atom bomb detonated. And he—he didn't even see she was furious. That made her even angrier. Caroline slammed her coffee cup down.

"Go play outside!"

Both father and son stood up.

Caroline said, "I meant Jeffrey." Junior sat down again.

Junior said, "He got the boat."

Caroline said, "I want a divorce."

Junior said, "What? You can't divorce me! I'm the president!"

Caroline said, "It's a long time coming."

Junior said, "Right! Before, you always said it was too quick!"

Caroline said, "I've found someone new."

Junior said, "Who? Who is it?"

Caroline said, "What difference does it make?"

Junior said, "Tell me, so I can go do the manly thing and gun him down!"

Caroline said, "It really doesn't matter who it is."

Junior said, "Do I know him?"

Caroline said, "Yes."

Junior said, "Is it Chet?"

Caroline said, "No."

Junior said, "Chet's gay."

Caroline said, "So I've heard."

Junior said, "Well, tell me. I can take it. I'm a grown up."

Caroline said, "It's the vice president."

Junior said, "The vice president! Damn! Which one? I bet it was Rod!"

Caroline said, "It wasn't Rod. It was Fang!"

Junior said, "Fang! No! You can't leave me for a dog!" Junior threw a fit, rolling around the floor like Shemp.

"And with your little whore."

"What? What!"

"Kennedy."

"You slept with Kennedy? Well, I guess that makes her OUR little whore."

Caroline shrugged.

"You were with both of them? A three-way? I've never gotten a three-way, and I said I wanted one. Well, it probably wasn't much fun since you only lie there, I mean, it's not like you do anything oral."

"I did," Caroline said.

"You did what?"

"I did... have oral intercourse," Caroline said. She wanted to look down, find her purse, leave, but she did none of those things and, instead, looked Junior right in the eyes.

"Oh man! I'm your husband, it should've been me. All I ever get is those rubber gloves. Who got it? Him or her?"

"Both of them," she said.

"What?" Life was often shocking for Junior. But this was too much. His entire marriage he'd begged Caroline to go oral on

238

him, and she would barely put her eyes on him, much less her mouth.

"I had him. She had me. He had me. I did her."

"It was a regular orgy, wasn't it?" Junior felt tears coming to his eyes. He was angry, but he hadn't expected to get all emotional. He thought about those big machines that crush cars into a little cube. That's what he did with his feelings, stopping the waterworks before the presidential drama hit the floodgates.

"And now I want a divorce. I want to be with Tip. And Fang."

One of the servers slipped from the table and went to the bathroom. He locked the door, shut the small ventilation window, then dialed his cell. "Irma? Have I got a story for you!" In an instant, the electronic tabloids hit—Worthys' Divorce! First Lady Files! First Lady Flips for Fang! Vice President her Secret Lover!

Junior returned to the table wearing a sweat suit. "Are you going to give me a divorce?" Caroline asked.

"No, I'm going on a jog."

Junior wandered out to the grounds where the paparazzi waited behind the bushes until they spotted him and hit the ground running. Junior jogged with his fingers in his ears while the paps chased close behind.

"Mr. President! Mr. President! Is it true the First Lady is divorcing you?"

Junior said, "I can't hear you!"

From a doorway, Murphy had watched the whole Junior and Caroline show. "What an idiot," he said.

Jim Donaldson walked up behind him. "What's worse? His stupidity or your phony snake oil act." Donaldson was done counting on one assassin. He needed multiple players.

Murphy batted his eyes and said in his Blanche voice, "Why, Jim, darlin', I have no clue what you are speakin' of."

Donaldson said, "You know exactly what I mean."

Murphy continued as Blanche, "I do believe you were banished from the White House."

Donaldson said, "Let them throw me out."

Murphy continued as Blanche, "You know, I was in love with a boy once. A boy like you. A sensitive boy. And then I hear that music playin' and then KA-BOOM!" He switched to his regular, Murphy voice. "There's that gunshot."

"Knock off that lousy drag act. I need you, Murphy."

Murphy said, "If you need me, maybe I better pump up the drag act."

"Not for me. For Junior."

Murphy said, "Christ, Jim, even I have my limits."

"I don't want you to have sex with him."

Murphy said, "Then what?"

Donaldson stood in the doorway for a moment. He said nothing. Finally, his mouth opened, and he said, "Look Murphy, I hate you."

"I hate you back."

"Want to work together?"

"Okay. What did you have in mind?"

"Junior. I want you to kill him."

Murphy said, "Are you out of your mind?

Donaldson said, "You won't do it. Rod will."

Murphy said, "I'd go to jail."

"Go to jail? You'd be a hero. You'd get a medal. Then you'd be president. You wouldn't be held responsible, Rod would."

Murphy said, "What's in it for you?"

Donaldson said, "I get my job back."

Murphy said, "Okay."

Donaldson hesitated then spoke again. "And..."

Murphy said, "And what?"

Donaldson said, "You send that goddamn Press Secretary to some queer-hating country."

Murphy said, "That's easy. I don't need to send him anywhere. He's already in the United States."

Donaldson said, "Okay, Murph. I'm depending on you."

Murphy said, "Uh huh. And what if I won't?"

"You've got to do it. This is the only chance of saving this country."

Murphy said, "Hmm. I have a videotape you may be interested in. How about, instead of killing Junior, we wait it out and elect someone else?"

"We may not last that long. You're the only one who can do it, Tip. You're truly a great American."

Murphy said in his Blanche voice, "Thank you, Jim. I have always depended upon the kindness of bullshitters." Then Murphy's voice changed, and Donaldson didn't know who he was trying to be.
Murphy said, "It is a far, far better thing that I do, than I have ever done."

"Who's that?" asked Donaldson

"Dickens, asshole."

They both laughed.

Chapter 23

Why had he wasted any money on Fat Ass? He could cause plenty of damage without a retainer and per diem. Tip was useless. Tip had handed over the tape and it turned out this tech stuff was easy. The dirty dreadhead, Everett, had disappeared. Two hundred bucks down the drain. Donaldson logged on. He had built a junky homegrown web page. It looked like a teenage kid had made it—loud, green and blue background, ugly yellow and red fonts that changed with every word. It was exactly what he wanted. He typed, Doin the NaStiE—is she WoRtHy? He highlighted the sentence then linked it to the digital clip. Donaldson already made several copies of the tape and put them in the mail to some choice recipients, just in case people didn't see the website. Word was out. Now they would have pictures.

Fletcher Worthy was doing his daily march through the Oval Office. Chet watched him. Fletcher said, "You're not nominated son, and you're failing in the polls."

"I've got bigger problems than that."

"I've got an idea, son. You have a debate."

"I don't think I'm very good at that."

"With me."

"With you? Why would I debate my Dad?"

"It's a setup. I'll make sure you look good. We'll make sure you win."

"A setup! I debate my Dad! What do you think, Chet?"

"I'm afraid this is going to explode like a cartoon cigar," Chet said.

"It's a simple idea, yet brilliant. You'll debate me, we'll have you totally prepared, you'll win, look like a hero, and the GOP will have to select you as their candidate."

"I debate my own Dad."

"Just think of it as sitting around the dinner table."

"You mean I'm going to have to debate my own Dad AND I'm going to have to eat a salad?"

"Like, here's a tactic. Don't argue with me. Agree with me. Thank me for everything I've ever done. You'll look smart. Like a diplomat. People will love you."

244

"Great idea, Dad. Chet, let's set up this debate."

Chet hesitated. "I don't think this is a good idea."

"Just do it, Chet."

The sound of her voice was harsh. "What do you think you're doing?"

"What?"

"Are you out of your mind? Are you out of your freaking mind?"

"Who is this?"

"You know exactly who this is. Caroline Worthy."

"Caroline!" Donaldson said. "Good to hear from you. What seems to be the trouble?"

"That sex tape!" Several people turned and looked at her. She whispered, "The sex tape. It's all over the Internet. It's everywhere! And my hair looks terrible."

"I've heard. It's awful. I don't know who would do such a thing. Why did you let Tip tape that stuff? I tell yah, he makes Bill Clinton look like a choir boy. And you! You must have had to see a chiropractor after all that."

"Tip told me it was you. He gave you the tape."

"Moi? How would I ever do such a thing! I barely use a computer. He's just trying to get out of this. That guy's got some real problems. I should've warned you before

245

you got involved with him. And it wasn't one of his personalities. It was him. And I thought you wanted people to know about it."

"I wanted people to know about it, but I didn't want my hair to look like... crap! And none of this is getting my husband out of office!"

Chet hesitated. More than anything in the world, he wanted to go in. And more than anything in the world, he didn't. "Come on!!" Kennedy said. Her voice roared with impatience. Chet pulled on the door handle, the clunking sound of it opening, like cocking a gun. Did the bar have to be called "The White Swallow?" Couldn't there be a classier place? Couldn't they have gone to the Side Car? Kennedy didn't have any issues with him being gay and she'd convinced him to go to this bar. He should have stayed home, but he was already inside and it was dark. And hot. A relief. No one could recognize him here. Gawd, they could barely make out his silhouette!

He was his son, after all, but he was also a little bitch. Did he even like his own son? The jury was out. But it didn't really matter. He would have a debate with his own son. And before it was over, his son would be packing his bags and he, Fletcher Worthy, would be the Republican nominee for president. The debate would be history, and so would his son.

Jim Donaldson searched through his dresser drawers. He had gathered a small pile of weapons for Tip. He hoped Tip could do it, but just in case, he would play all angles. He would not fail. He started throwing things from the dresser.

"...watched these schmoozers come and go. Patched up their blunders like you wouldn't believe. I've had to take their crap... and then I've put it in a fancy wrapper and sold it to the American People. These idiots don't know what it takes to be a leader. If anyone should be running this country, it's me." Then he found it. It was almost as if it had been looking for him too. A gun. His gun. A Beretta M9 in a black Bruniton finish. Okay, Murphy, I'll get you every weapon you need, and I'm keeping this one for myself. He placed the gun inside his jacket.

"First, I'm gonna kill that useless dread-headed monster." Donaldson picked up a news clipping of Junior. "Then I'm gonna show 'em why the first six letters of assassinate are Double-ASS." He crumpled the news clipping and tossed it on the floor.

She gave in and saw him again, but she'd given him an ultimatum. If he wanted her back, he needed to give up this silly act, marry her, retire, and move to Florida. He'd invited her for an intimate dinner, but it wasn't what she had expected. She scraped her fork on the plate. She looked across the table at Tip. He wore a black slip and heels. He could've at least put on a dress.

"Okay, I'm giving it up."

"You're giving what up?"

"The drag act. The multiples. Our relationship is more important."

Wanda couldn't believe it. She let out a long breath. "I'm so glad you've decided to come clean with this business. Tell the world the truth."

"Hmmm. Well, I don't know if the truth is the best way to go. I was thinking miracle cure. Maybe an evangelical minister—then I could pull the fundamentalists on my team. I mean, I can't just tell the truth. I don't want to look like a nut."

Wanda would have liked the truth, but what difference did it make? This ridiculous nightmare would be over. "Well, any way you do it, I'm just glad it'll be over. So, are you thinking... this weekend?"

Murphy frowned, shaking his head. He swallowed a bite then said, "I'm thinking right after I finish my road tour. Hey, what do you think of this? I'm Norman. Norman Desmond. Norma Desmond's grandson." Murphy went into his imitation, "You used to be big! I am big! It's the residuals that got small! I'm ready for my close-up, Mr. Spielberg." Tip was pleased with himself. He held his hands out for her approval. "Huh? Huh?"

Wanda couldn't believe it. "What?"

Murphy said, "It's no big deal. Just one last fling. A road trip. The money's good, and I'll get to see the country."

"Tip, you're impossible!"

Murphy said, "Oh, and there's this small bit part in a movie."

Wanda threw her napkin on the floor. "I've had it. I don't want to see you anymore, Tip." She stood up to go. He grabbed her arm and pulled her back down into the chair.

Murphy said, "Wanda, wait. I've worked in politics my whole life. The most recognition I've ever had was when I sponsored that crime bill. And it didn't pass."

"So, things haven't been perfect. At least you had some dignity."

Murphy stood up and straightened his slip then said, "What's Washington got to do with dignity? Now I'm on top. Now I'm somebody!"

"You're somebody all right. The most famous nutcase in town."

Murphy said, "Nutcase! Everyone knows who I am. People treat me with respect. People like me."

"Is that why you came here? To be liked?"

Murphy said, "Sure I dreamed of change… but that was a long time ago. Don't try and rub my face in stinkin' values!"

Wanda stood up again. "I've got to go."

Murphy said, "It's only a game, Wanda. And while I'm hot, I'm gonna play it for all it's worth. I can stop anytime."

"Sure. That's what they say about heroin."

She grabbed her purse and walked out the door. Murphy ran after her but stopped at the door. He was ready to grab the handle, instead he embraced himself, nuzzling the fabric of his slip.

The debate was set. Everyone had been against it. The party was against it, the networks were against it, the advisors were against it. But it was set. The audience had been bribed with a goodie bag. The lights were blinding, and Fletcher stood behind one podium, Junior behind the other. The moderator set the ground rules, and Junior broke in, "I just wanna say, I'm gonna be the best president ever! I want all the people to love me! And I'm gonna make Hawaii the 51st state! That place rocks!"

Fletcher shook his head "It already IS a state! Idiot. Boy, you've never worked hard, you're unprepared, and you don't really care about the citizens of the United States. How are you gonna be a decent president?"

"My lack of experience is... what was I saying? Anyway, I don't really see that as a problem. How hard can it be?"

The moderator trudged on. "We'll begin with opening statements. Each speaker will have one minute. Let's start with Fletcher Worthy."

Fletcher Worthy adjust his cowboy hat. "First, I'd like to start with an apology. I'm sorry I ever had you, son. I apologize to the whole country." The audience gasped. Junior nodded his head, knowing somehow this would lead to him winning. "I know our country has advanced ADD and can't remember the past from week to week but let me remind you. You wanted to impeach this kid of mine. He started riots, he insulted dignitaries, we're on the brink of war, AND he decapitated Abraham Lincoln." The audience became restless as they recalled Junior's transgressions. "My son's an idiot. And we can't have an idiot running this country. We need a real leader. We need me." And with that, Fletcher stopped.

"President Worthy," the moderator said indicating it was Junior's turn. Junior didn't understand his Dad's strategy, but he had his speech ready.

"I was lucky, you know. My real father died serving our country. All I have left of my real father is the medal he earned dying for our freedom." Junior opened his jacket and flashed the medal. "The indigo heart."

People in the audience looked at each other, then yelled to Junior, "There is no indigo heart!" They were laughing. Junior could hear it. They were laughing at him. They were laughing at him and his father and his father's medal.

Fletcher didn't seem to have any problem with this. He gulped down half a glass of water, turned to Junior and said, "Oh yeah, you know how I told you your father died in the military?"

"Yes."

"That was a lie."

Junior didn't move, but he staggered. "What?"

"I could see you were going to be a mama's boy, and I knew I had to do something to toughen you up."

Someone from the crowd yelled, "Too bad it didn't work!"

"So I lied. I told you that you were adopted."

"You what? You told... you told me I was adopted."

"I had to."

"So I'm not adopted? So you're... you're my real Daddy?"

"Yes, Junior."

"Mom is my real Mom?"

"Yes. You didn't notice how much you looked like me?"

"But my name—Jerry Junior! Named after the war hero."

"Oh, I just named you that to mess with you."

"But, Daddy, the medal! The indigo heart."

"Oh yeah. That was a cufflink. Just something I picked up at Monkey Wards."

"A cufflink? Monkey Wards! Daddy!"

"Yeah, I soldered it on a pin back."

The medal, the medal he'd worn all those years, the indigo heart, was a fake. His history was a lie. His hero father a sham. He was as plain as anyone else.

"You are my real son. And I'm telling you that you are my real son, just so I can disown you. And I'm disowning you right now."

Junior felt like he was going to fall over. He could feel himself wobble, back to front, then side to side. Lights were glaring and flashbulbs popping, and he thought he was going to pass out. He turned to look for Chet or Caroline or Kennedy or anybody, but the whole mass was spinning and spinning. He clenched the podium for a few seconds, then turned and ran.

"That's what you can expect," said Fletcher to the cameras. "When things get tough, the big baby runs."

Jedidiah Butts sat at his desk in his home office. A small thirteen- inch TV at full volume blasted the debate. As Junior folded like a lawn chair, Butts thought of the

253

watch. Then he thought of his own father, the cracks on his father's hands and the dirt in his fingernails from doing hard labor, and his mother, praying by the light of the moon. He remembered his Uncle Dez, the smiling face that brought the second-hand bike. His dog, Boomer. He could feel the heavy black fabric of his first graduation gown. His son. His wife. Losing his son. Losing his wife. The snow globe. Then he thought about the watch. The world chiseled into gold. The feel and the sound of winding it and slipping it into his vest pocket. Time, it slips away faster than a shy child. His mother, giving him the watch. Planet Earth carved into the hues of gold, brown, and flaxen, Planet Earth in his pocket. The smoothness where the etching had worn away. The watch, rotating like the planet, golden, carved, rotating, Planet Earth. The watch. The beautiful, beautiful watch. The watch that he could hold in his hand like it was the entire world. His beautiful, beautiful watch. Butts placed his head down on the desk and died.

Chapter 24

Junior ran out the double doors of the studio. The Secret Service hadn't been prepared for him to bolt, but they were hot on his heels. The streets were crowded. He walked quickly and tried to blend in with the crowd. He ducked into a dry-cleaning store and hid in the suits. The Secret Service hadn't seen him go through the door, they looked through the window, saw hundreds of suits on a rack and kept running. The woman who ran the shop had a horrified look on her face.

"Are you—?"

He popped out from the suits and yelled, "No!" then hid again. A woman came in.

"Hi, Mellie. I'm in a rush—left the car running and everything. Just want to pick up my stuff."

All Junior had to hear was "left the car running," and he was out the door. He saw the silver Jetta and jumped in. A four speed—damn! It had been two decades since he'd driven a stick. He sputtered out from the parking spot and drove away. Grand Theft Auto. He hoped the voters would understand.

Junior drove and drove and drove. At one point, he came to a stop light, put the car in neutral, then couldn't get it out of neutral. He jumped out of the car and ran. He had no idea where he was, but this neighborhood looked poor. "Spare change?" an old man leaning against a store called. "Spare change for food?" A group of teens were throwing something at another teen who was screaming in pain. Rocks? Maybe. The teens called the one boy a faggot. Wow, he hoped that wasn't how Chet felt when he talked about him being gay.

"Hey, Buddy, we need some help!" a car had broken down and a few people were trying to push it to the side of the road.

Junior ran over and got behind the car with the others. He'd never pushed a car before. As a matter of fact, he couldn't really remember helping anyone before. They pushed the car to the curb. "Why didn't you just call for a tow?"

"I can't pay for that."

"It's free. It's included in your insurance."

"I don't have insurance!" the man said. No insurance? Junior had never heard that before. "Well, thanks, Buddy!" the man said.

Junior walked away. No one had ever called him anything but Junior before. Well that was that. His father had disowned him. He would disown Junior. He wasn't Junior anymore. Junior was gone. From now on, he was Buddy.

He walked around the neighborhood. People were really suffering. He hadn't seen it before. People were hanging out, on corners or in front of houses. Why were people hanging out? They must not have jobs, and this area looked poor. He had thought when he first became president that maybe he could make a difference. He hadn't made a difference. He could have made jobs. He could have worked to end poverty. He could have made the world a better place. Was there still a chance? Could he make things better, even a little?

Junior wandered to a corner store and stood outside, near the trash cans. *The indigo heart!* He looked at it. Four and a half decades of possibilities had been wrapped up in that medal. Fantasies of what his father had looked like, how he had thrown himself on a grenade to save his entire platoon, how Junior might have been different if his father had been with him all along... and, damnit! He had been with him all along! Junior yanked the medal off his suit. He heard the pin break when he pulled. He hurled the medal as hard as he could into the trash can. He stood there for a moment, lost. Then he remembered. He reached into his pocket and took out Butts' watch. He opened it, then closed it. He carefully placed the watch in his breast pocket, replacing the medal. His hand touched it, then lingered for a second.

Two Secret Service men came running up behind him. They grabbed him at the elbow and scooped him up, his feet were walking forward without touching the ground. The Secret Service men tossed him into a limo.

"Junior, are you all right?"

"No."

"What's wrong?"

"It's Buddy now."

Junior rolled down the street. The Secret Service were used to Junior's droning on incomprehensibly during rides, but his time, he sat in silence, gazing out the window. He saw homeless men sitting outside a tent, so many people were suffering. He'd never noticed it before. He made a choice. He had to make a difference.

Junior was back in the Oval Office with Kennedy and Chet. They were both glad he came home safe, but there was no time for a happy reunion.

Chet said, "The Middle East crisis has reached its tipping point. I've called in Reed's top foreign advisors. This is a touchy situation, but with the right negotiators, we just might be able to avoid World War III."

Junior said, "I don't need those guys."

Chet said, "You need their experience. These are some of the most brilliant men in the world.

Junior said, "I can figure this out on my own. I can stop World War III."

Chet looked at Kennedy. "Talk some sense into him!"

This was the first time she'd been acknowledged as a member of the team, asked for input, asked to help. What would a white guy do? A white guy would agree with the boss, suck up to him, tell him he's brilliant and he can handle this himself. That's what a white guy would do. She opened her mouth. "I think you should listen to Reed's advisors."

Junior reached in his pocket, took out Butts' watch. Opened it. Looked at it. Put it back in his pocket. "Okay, I'll listen to the advisors. I have to make things better for everyone!"

Chet breathed out a sigh of relief. "You did it, Kennedy!"

I did? she thought. *Yeah. Yeah, I did.*

Chet said, "I'll coordinate the advisors. And I'll set up a meeting!"

Donaldson stood in Murphy's apartment as the news blared on TV in the background. Donaldson dumped off various equipment—utility belt, blackjack, harpoon gun.

The newscaster said, "...as the world teeters on the brink of nuclear annihilation, there's still no action from the White house..."

Murphy said, "This clown has created a frickin' Armageddon!"

Donaldson said, "Okay, it's all here. A .357 mag, multiple magazines, this thing, and the harpoon gun you asked for."

Murphy said, "There's only one thing missing."

Donaldson said, "What?"

Murphy said, "Me. I won't do it."

Donaldson said, "You can't back out on me now!"

That's when the tube caught their attention. A somber reporter sat at the desk. "... and has threatened to use nuclear force."

A picture of Tip appeared on the screen. "Earlier today, it was revealed that the vice president's multiple personality diagnosis was a hoax." A piece of tape ran, featuring the young schoolgirl from the Geraldo show. The schoolgirl said, "Why did he do this to me? I believed him! I trusted him! Now my life is ruined!" She cried hysterically and was comforted by her mother. The tape switched to protesters outside the White House carrying signs that read "Murphy is a Bad Tip." "Multiple Personalities are no joke. I think so too." "Fry, Murphy, Fry!"

The reporter continued. "Protesters gathered in front of the White House today. Vice President Murphy may face multiple charges including a libel suit filed by the Chicago Bulls. In an unrelated story, Murphy signed a deal for a guest appearance on the daytime drama, 'Turmoil At Dusk.'"

Murphy banged on the TV screen. He yelled, "Listen to me! Listen! You don't understand!"

Donaldson whispered into his phone. "I think you better come see Tip. It doesn't matter if you broke up. Hurry. He's losing it." Donaldson exited, taking a final, disgusted look at Murphy who was losing it, fighting with the reporter on TV.

"NO, Tip Murphy is not a hoax! He's a hero. A hero!"

Donaldson called as he walked out the door, "Don't lose it, Murphy. You've got to kill Junior."

Murphy was sweating and panting. "Yes." He stood up. "Where's my Molotov Cocktail? Where's my Molotov Cocktail!"

Chapter 25

Alone. It was night. He was alone in the Oval Office. It was a new feeling, but he was okay. He wasn't exactly sure what he was going to say. He put his hand on the watch, he could feel it through his suit, then Junior faced the cameras. "My fellow Americans, first, I want to tell you, I have a new name—Buddy. And now, we stand on the verge of a nuclear catastrophe. I haven't done a great job up to this point. But tonight, I saw suffering... and I don't want people to suffer. I want to make things better. I'll do my best to stop this war."

Wanda used her key to let herself in. The night was still. There was no sound in the apartment. No music. No TV. No hello from Tip. She walked through the small rooms then saw Tip, sitting on the bed. He had his back to her, looking out the window, focused on the full moon.

"There's something about the moon that always reflects the truth. Don't you think?" He turned to her, and his under eyes seemed to have been circled with red. He looked around, found his drink, then emptied it. Wanda walked toward the bed.

Murphy said, "Thanks for coming over.

Wanda said, "What are you doing?"

"Looking at the moon.

Wanda tried to make a joke. "Do you see the man in the moon?"

Murphy said, "Yes. Look at him. Look at him, locked in his big white orb of light. No way out. Only one destiny. Look, at him, Wanda. The man in the moon is in pain!"

Wanda moved to the window. She looked out, not sure what to say or do. "What do you mean?"

Murphy said, "Look. Can't you see? It looks like he's screaming or squirming. He's in horrible, indescribable pain!"

He's not the only one, Wanda thought. She thought of her husband, near the end. So wigged out on painkillers there was no difference between reality and hallucinations. She hadn't thought of her husband's hallucinations in a long, long time.

Murphy said, "Is there any more scotch?"

263

"Tip, you need to snap out of it."

"I don't need to snap out of anything!" She could hear his teeth grinding as he said it, and at the end of the sentence, he threw his empty glass against the wall. It didn't shatter, just broke into a few solid pieces and dropped to the floor.

"So, what are you gonna do? Are you gonna help Junior fix this mess? Or do you want to keep being Blanche and Rod and Fang?"

Murphy said, "It's not my problem."

Wanda stood right in front of him. "It is your problem. It's your country. It's your world. You have the chance to stop a nuclear war. Being a leader is about rising out of these ashes and leading people to a better life. Not just American people—all people."

Murphy said, "You sound like a campaign speech."

She continued, "You know Junior can't handle this. But you can. Do you want to keep the world from committing suicide?"

Murphy said, "Maybe it should commit suicide. Maybe we'd all be better off."

"I can't believe you're saying that. This is your crucial moment. Are you going to come through?"

Tip looked back at the moon.

Wanda tried to block the window. "Murphy, listen to me."

Murphy turned away from Wanda and looked at the equipment Donaldson left. He picked up the harpoon gun. "The name's Rod," he said.

Wanda moved in front of him again. "The name's not Rod. Your name is Murphy!"

Murphy said, "Murphy's dead. I killed him."

Wanda's voice was wavering. "You're losing your senses!"

Murphy used his Rod voice, "There's a lesson, you know. Play with fire, and you're bound to get burned."

Murphy stood up, and Wanda had to move aside. It was as if he didn't even see her. He strapped the utility belt on and grabbed up the equipment. He secured the harpoon gun in the belt, checked to see he had a few harpoons.

"What are you doing?"

Murphy said now in his Blanche voice, "Get away from this city, Stella, Stella! Stella for star! Run as far as you can. And trust me—stay away from the light!"

Murphy grabbed the bat-hook Donaldson had left, tossed it out the window and tethered down the line. How exciting it was to watch a taut, twenty-year old athlete ride the line, but Murphy, in his fifties with a paunchy beer gut, made a rather frightening sight. He had latched onto the wire and seemed to weigh it down. He slowly slid across the skyline, haphazardly tossing firebombs along his way. Wanda watched from the window and thought, *he looks like a middle-aged Tinkerbell of Terrorism.*

Junior was alone. The speech was over. He stood in the Oval Office holding his phone. He was going to call someone, but who? Chet? No. Kennedy? No. His traitor of a father? No. Who? Who? Who? Right then, Murphy crashed through the window. He landed in a heap on the floor, covered with glass. Security alarms blared.

Junior said, "Oh good, Murphy. I was just gonna call you."

"It's Rod."

"Oh, you think you're Rod?"

With grit in his sneer and a glare in his eye, Murphy looked at Junior. "I don't think I'm Rod. I am Rod." Murphy pulled out the harpoon gun and loaded a spear.

Junior said, "What's that?"

Murphy said, "It's a harpoon gun."

Junior said, "You idiot! There aren't any harpoons in here!"

Murphy said, "I'm gonna use it to kill you."

Junior said, "Look, if this is about you and Caroline, we can work something out. I mean, you can have the slut."

Murphy said, "I don't give a damn about Caroline."

Junior said, "Then there's a chance she and I can work things out!"

Murphy said, "Yeah, but you're gonna have to negotiate from six feet under!" Murphy fired the gun. The harpoon spear flew. It missed Junior and sunk deep into the heart of a picture of George Washington. Murphy said, "Damn! The sight is off!" He should've known that Donaldson would give him second rate equipment.

Junior pulled the harpoon out of the picture. The spear had three jagged heads on it. "You could kill a guy with something like—Yikes!"

Murphy reloaded and tried to get a bead on Junior. Junior ran down the hall yelling, "Geez, Murphy! Why couldn't you just shoot me with a handgun!"

Murphy said, "And miss the pleasure of taking you out with this whaling weapon? Seeing your blubber dangling on this jagged shish-kabob? No dice." A Secret Serviceman ran into the hall. One look at the harpoon gun and he ran out again.

Junior ran into a dead end. He stood with his back against the wall. Murphy lined Junior up in the sight. The crosshairs centered right on Junior's scared shitless expression. Murphy said, "You look just like a deer caught in the headlights... and that's exactly where I want you." Murphy unloaded the second spear. The harpoon sliced Junior's hair, leaving a clean part.

Junior said, "Wow, I've been trying to part my hair like that since I was thirty! Nice work. That's it. Murphy, if you promise not to shoot me, I'll give you a big fat bonus!"

Murphy said, "Okay. I promise. Let's shake on it."

"That's what I'm best at! Shaking hands." Junior walked over to shake hands with Murphy. Murphy quickly reloaded the harpoon gun and shot Junior in the foot. Junior bounced around the room like a kangaroo on speed. Junior said, "This reminds me of a story. The lion with the thorn in his paw. Did the lion need surgery? I've got to get to the hospital."

Murphy said, "I never knew it would be so hard to kill an idiot." But now it would be easy. He was wounded. If he ran, he couldn't run far, and he couldn't run fast. Murphy reached for another harpoon—damn! He had spent them all. He started looking through his arsenal and found what he thought was a small flamethrower. He pressed the button and the air was underlined with fire. Yep. Flamethrower.

Looking for another weapon had given the weasel a chance to get away. He'd ducked from the dead end and headed back down the hallway. Murphy had been a bit too obsessed with the flame. He started to run. Dammit, even with a bad foot, Junior Worthy was faster than he was, but Junior couldn't decide which way to go, and Murphy caught up with him, trapped in the Oval Office. Junior had climbed on the desk. Murphy locked the door. He pushed a large chair in front of the door. He clicked on the flamethrower. The smell! Propane! It smelled like power! He walked toward Junior, step by step by step.

"Okay, okay, whatever you want! I just don't want a hot foot! You want to be president? It's all yours. You want Caroline? Take her! Just don't hurt me!"

Murphy moved to the coolness, the air drifting through where he'd crashed through the window. The breeze. It was icy. The propane. The smell. Where was that Molotov Cocktail? He needed it now. Oh yeah. It was at his side, in a sling. He lifted it, ignited it, tossed it, and it exploded. "Freedom!" He yelled. "Freeeeeeeeeeeee-dumb!" Outside the window he could see—who were they? Press, maybe? Security? Could they see the tongue licking madly from the flamethrower? The long, fiery tongue... was it love trapped inside? Licking, lapping, rolling. It wanted free. It wanted freedom. He pressed the flame against the cream-colored drapes, and it raced up the threads. He had set it free. He had won. The flames curved around the bay window and engulfed him. He cackled wildly as the firestorm swirled. The sound of it. That's what they mean when a fire roars. The smell now—not fuel, smoke. It wasn't powerful, more sleepy. Murphy yawned. The fire danced the ballet with him, forward, forward, back, and he thought of the

269

Nutcracker Suite as he dropped to the floor, just enough light to see Junior push the chair and run down the hall.

Junior saw her. "Kennedy!"

"Yeah, it's me. I saw what you said. You did right, Junior. I mean Buddy!"

"You called me Buddy! Thanks for telling me to listen to the advisors."

"It's okay. Even when I try to do what whitey would do, I can't. I'm not whitey, and I never will be.

"Yes to whatever you're talking about."

"I guess I'm gonna have to be happy being myself."

"And I like it that way." He kissed her.

"I like making out as much as anybody, but maybe we should get out of here while we're still alive. Plus, your foot is pretty bloody." Smoke was filling the hall. As they moved, Donaldson appeared from the shadows. Donaldson grabbed Kennedy, holding the barrel of his Beretta to her head.

"How do you like it now, Junior? Your concubine has become your damsel in distress."

"Damsel in distress, my ass!" said Kennedy. She stomped on Donaldson's foot, then elbowed him in the gut. He dropped his grip on her and doubled over, then she smashed him on the head. She grabbed for his gun, but he kicked her in the stomach, and she fell to the ground.

"That wasn't nice. Oh, and by the way, now I'm going by Buddy."

Then, just like that, Everett entered. None of them had heard or seen him, he just walked into the hall. He wore the same clothes as when Donaldson had made his down payment. He had a deranged look in his eye. He pulled out a .45 and held it at Junior.

"Boy, everyone wants a piece of me! Too bad you weren't here earlier. You coulda killed Tip Murphy."

"Kill Tip Murphy," Everett said. His brain was fucked up, but it registered. He knew that name. Tip Murphy. Where had he heard it? "Don't tell anyone it was me—Tip Murphy." Tip Murphy, Tip Murphy. He aimed the gun on the only Tip Murphy he'd ever known. He pulled back his index finger, the gun fired and knocked Everett back up against the wall. Donaldson was hit in the heart. He flew back then landed. Everett got up, helped himself to Donaldson's wallet and gun. He took out the license, looked at it, at Donaldson, then said, "Ah, shit! He's not Tip Murphy!" With cash in hand, Everett crashed through the window and ran. Kennedy held Junior. "Let's get the hell out of here!" They both ran for their lives.

Chapter 26

Sunlight peeked through the window. Murphy, dressed in drag as Blanche, sat in a chair near the window. She was highly agitated. She pulled the shades. She seemed fragile. With a shaking hand, Murphy applied more lipstick as his head bobbed helplessly. The lipstick traveled around the outline of her lips. An assistant ducked his head through the door.

The assistant said, "It's almost time."

Murphy spoke as Blanche. "I can't let them see me like this, I just can't."

"You look fine." The assistant crossed the room and pulled the shade cord, popping them open and blasting the sun into the room.

Murphy continued in the Blanche voice. "Please! That glaring light! It's so brutal!"

Dr. Patel entered quietly. He was in his early sixties and wore a gray suit and black tie. The attendant nodded with a look of both sadness and resignation. "Hello, Blanche," said the doctor. He picked up Murphy's hand and took his pulse.

"Oh, sir, you must be my escort."

The doctor said, "Yes, Blanche. Yes I am."

"It's been so long since I've had a gentleman caller. And such a handsome suitor!" She allowed the doctor to escort her. "Did I ever tell you about my coming out party? It was lovely, but also a bit of a drag... You know I have always depended upon the kindness of... of... kind people! Yes, that's it, the kindness of kind people! Especially kind men."

Murphy sauntered to the door. Outside, she could hear a commotion. She asked the doctor, "What's that?"

"It's the press, Blanche."

"The press! Oh, the press! They love me!" She looked at the attendant and said to him, "Be a dear and carry my bag."

The doctor opened the door, and as he did, three photographers fell into the apartment. "Blanche! Blanche! Blanche!" It seemed ten thousand men were calling her name, begging for her to look their way, to grace them with her smile, just like at her debutante ball.

She took a few tenuous steps then popped open a parasol. "The light, you know. A girl's got to be careful."

The faces were a swirl, but she could hear them say, "She was quite a looker," and "There'll never be another one like her," and "We love you Blanche!"

She waved her hanky with her free hand and said, "I love you too, boys! I love all of you!" She climbed into the waiting car. It was odd, almost a truck. White with a thick red stripe and filled to the gills with medical equipment. This must be one of those SUVs she'd heard about. They had a fainting couch for her—she was going to get to lie down! Now this was a man who understood a girl's frazzled nerves. Two men helped Blanche onto the fainting couch and buckled her in. She waved the queen's wave as the suitor attached something to her other wrist. It must be a corsage! She'd look in a minute, but someone outside caught her eye. A woman, middle aged, with mousy brown hair and glasses. The look of a librarian. She looked familiar. Oh, but didn't they all. She was off to another party, the social event of the season, with her gentleman caller, as the doors closed, she looked down for the corsage.

Junior had demanded the negotiations be public. On the East Lawn. Chet had argued against it—it wasn't the

Easter Egg Roll for God's sake. Kennedy and Caroline stood by in support. Junior was on crutches, his harpooned foot wrapped. Congressman Butts was gone, but he had told Junior to listen to the people. Junior took a glance at the watch. All the answers were in the watch. And all the answers were in Junior. And all the answers were in everyone. He knew he could make this all work out. Junior wound the watch and put it back in his inner suit pocket.

"What are their names?" Chet asked.

"I thought YOU knew!" said Junior.

Chet decided then and there to up his blood pressure meds. "I DO know. I want to make sure you don't embarrass us by messing up their names."

"Oh... well, I can't remember all that! I'll just call them by my name. That one's Buddy Two and he's Buddy Three."

"Just call them both sir."

Junior sat between the two Middle East Leaders. Press and citizens had gathered to observe Junior's deft negotiation skills. Junior said, "You've got to think about the bigger picture."

Buddy Two said, "I can't let my people suffer under their hands."

Junior said, "It's not just your people, you've got to think about the whole world! That's what I'm trying to do."

Buddy Three said, "We will never deal with them. They are evil! Talks adjourned!"

Junior said, "Oh come on now. Look at Kennedy and me, we're totally different, and we're able to get along. We even have sex. And she's even done my wife. Everything's cool in America." The press went nuts, shooting pictures of Kennedy. Caroline's smile dissolved. Junior said, "I'm not saying you guys need to have sex or anything, just not blow up the world. It's a nice planet, don't you think."

Buddy Two said, "I agree to nothing!"

Buddy Three yelled, "He must concede."

Junior said, "Look, you guys, it's like this." He grabbed them both by the collar and smacked their heads together. It sounded like the cue ball cracking the eight. Junior said, "Now do you get it?"

Buddy Two said, "Ow. You'll pay for that, Junior! I mean Buddy!"

Buddy Three added, "But he has a point. If that hurt, think what the bomb will feel like."

Buddy Two leaned back in his chair, chin in hand. Then he said, "Hmmm... it would hurt bad... and we would destroy the rain forests, deplete our resources, kill off all of humanity, and start a nuclear winter that'll make this place look like Santa's Workshop. Buddy, you've knocked some sense into both of us!"

Buddy Two said to Buddy Three, "I believe I can get along with you, it won't be easy, but somehow, we can find a way. However, I'm not interested in having sex with you. But how about him?" Buddy Three pointed at Chet.

That was a no-brainer. Junior told him, "Oh yeah, he's available. Just sign this peace pact first. Then we can just all have sex with whoever we want, because this is America, land of the free! Yippee!" Junior inked his name and wondered what those two boys would do together under the sheets. He wondered what it must feel like to kiss someone with a mustache. He should've told Caroline not to wax her lip one month so he could have found out, but the crowd was applauding, and he forgot about putting his mouth on a hairy upper lip.

Junior said, "Whaddya know? I did it, Kennedy! And you helped!"

Kennedy said, "You've saved the world!"

Junior said, "I had a feeling I might. Well, do you think the GOP will change their mind and nominate me for re-election?"

"Oh hell no. Junior, I mean Buddy, you're dumb as dogshit."

"But I learned something! I learned there's value in serving others. And I learned I should have been doing something as president instead of just trying to keep the job. I learned a whole lot."

"Well, so what. It doesn't mean you know how to be a leader. And the American people, they may be stupid, but they're not idiots. They don't want a big ding-dong for president."

"You know what. You're right. I don't think I'd vote for me either. Hey, let's go get a root beer float!"

Kennedy smiled at him. "Good idea, Buddy. Good idea."

Also by BK Wells

Funny Money

AJ Billingsley needs cash and she needs it now. If she doesn't come up with money for her past rent, she'll be evicted, and so will her roommate, Kim. Together, with their drag queen friend, they hatch a crazy plan to storm the San Francisco Mint and steal enough fresh cash to guarantee their happily ever after. Unfortunately, they didn't consider the reinforced concrete building, the electric fence, or the 850,000 participants of the 2004 San Francisco Pride Parade.

Made in the USA
Columbia, SC
22 October 2020